She swallowed. 'I should go.' Her voice emerged as a tremulous whisper.

'Why not stay?'

There must be a good reason. Probably dozens. But his sexy smile decimated her ability to think logically.

Dimitri's voice thickened with desire. He did not understand what it was about this woman that made his body ache? All he knew was that Louise was like a fever in his blood, and the only cure was to possess her and find the sweet satiation his body craved.

He pulled her into his arms and his heart slammed against his ribs when he felt the tips of her nipples pressed against his chest. 'I want to take you to bed and undress you, slowly. I want to lay you down and kiss every inch of you—,' he whispered in her ear. 'And then I want to take you and make you mine, and give you more pleasure than you've ever had with any other man.'

Chantelle Shaw lives on the Kent coast, five minutes from the sea, and does much of her thinking about the characters in her books while walking on the beach. She's been an avid reader from an early age. Her schoolfriends used to hide their books when she visited—but Chantelle would retreat into her own world, and still writes stories in her head all the time.

Chantelle has been blissfully married to her own tall, dark and very patient hero for over twenty years, and has six children. She began to read Mills & Boon® as a teenager, and throughout the years of being a stay-at-home mum to her brood found romantic fiction helped her to stay sane! She enjoys reading and writing about strong-willed, feisty women, and even stronger-willed sexy heroes. Chantelle is at her happiest when writing. She is particularly inspired while cooking dinner, which unfortunately results in a lot of culinary disasters! She also loves gardening, walking, and eating chocolate (followed by more walking!). Catch up with Chantelle's latest news on her website: www.chantelleshaw.com

Recent titles by the same author:

BEHIND THE CASTELLO DOORS
A DANGEROUS INFATUATION
AFTER THE GREEK AFFAIR
THE ULTIMATE RISK

THE GREEK'S ACQUISITION

BY
CHANTELLE SHAW

First published in Great Britain 2012
by Mills & Boon, an imprint of Harlequin (UK) Limited.
Harlequin (UK) Limited, Eton House, 18-24 Paradise Road,
Richmond, Surrey TW9 1SR

© Chantelle Shaw 2012

ISBN: 978 0 263 89111 9

Harlequin (UK) policy is to use papers that are natural, renewable and recyclable products and made from wood grown in sustainable forests. The logging and manufacturing process conform to the legal environmental regulations of the country of origin.

Printed and bound in Spain
by Blackprint CPI, Barcelona

THE GREEK'S ACQUISITION

CHAPTER ONE

ATHENS at two-thirty on a summer's afternoon baked beneath a cloudless sky. A heat haze shimmered above the steps leading to the entrance of Kalakos Shipping, and the glare from the sun seemed to set the office block's bronze-tinted glass windows aflame.

The automatic doors parted smoothly as Louise approached them. Inside, the décor was minimalist chic, and the air-conditioned atmosphere was as hushed as a cathedral. Her stiletto heels reverberated excruciatingly loudly on the black marble floor as she walked up to the desk.

The receptionist was as elegant as the surroundings, impeccably dressed, her face discreetly made up. Her smile was politely enquiring.

'My name is Louise Frobisher. I'm here to see Dimitri Kalakos.' Louise spoke in fluent Greek. One of the only good things to come from her nomadic childhood was that she had developed a flair for learning languages.

The receptionist glanced at the appointments diary on the desk and her expertly shaped brows drew together in a faint frown.

'I'm sorry, but Mr Kalakos does not appear to have an appointment with you, Miss Frobisher.

Louise had planned for such a response. 'My visit is on

a personal, not a business matter. I assure you Mr Kalakos will be delighted to see me.'

The statement strained the truth thinner than an over-stretched elastic band, she acknowledged. But she had gambled on the fact that Dimitri had a reputation as a playboy, and that with luck the reception staff would believe she was one of his—according to the gossip columns—numerous mistresses. That was the reason she was wearing a skirt several inches shorter than she had ever worn before, and killer heels that made her legs look as if they went on for ever.

She had left her hair loose for once, instead of bundling it into a knot on top of her head, and she was wearing more make-up than usual; the smoky grey shadow on her eyelids emphasised the deep blue of her eyes and her scarlet lipgloss matched exactly the colour of her skirt and jacket. The diamond *fleur-de-lis* pendant suspended on a fine gold chain around her neck had been her grandmother's. It was the only piece of jewellery she owned, and she had chosen to wear it in the hope that if her *grand-mère*, Céline, was looking down on her she would send her good luck.

She had read somewhere that confidence tricksters were successful because they acted with absolute self-assurance. And so when the receptionist murmured that she would just check with Mr Kalakos's PA, Louise laughed and tossed her blond curls over her shoulders as she strolled towards the lift. Many years ago she had visited Kalakos Shipping, when her mother had been Kostas Kalakos's mistress, and she felt certain that Dimitri now occupied the luxurious office suite on the top floor of the building that had once been his father's.

'There's no question that Dimitri will want to see me. And I promise you he won't want us to be disturbed for quite a while,' she drawled.

The receptionist stared at her uncertainly, but to Louise's relief she made no further attempts to detain her. However, the moment the lift doors closed her bravado disappeared and she felt as awkward and unsure of herself as she had been at nineteen. She could recall as clearly as if it had happened yesterday the bitter confrontation that had taken place between her and Dimitri seven years ago, and the memory of his anger and her humiliation induced a churning sensation in the pit of her stomach.

The lift seemed horribly claustrophobic, but she took a deep breath and forced herself to stay calm. Dimitri represented her best hope of helping her mother, and it was vital she remained composed and in control of the emotions that had been see-sawing between apprehension and anticipation at the prospect of coming face to face with him again after all this time.

She should have expected that getting past his PA would prove to be far more difficult than the receptionist in the downstairs lobby. To give Aletha Pagnotis—her name was on the door of her office—due credit, she did phone through to her boss and relay Louise's request for five minutes of his time.

The request was met with a blank refusal.

'If you could tell me the reason for your visit, Miss Frobisher, then perhaps Mr Kalakos will reconsider his decision,' the PA murmured, after half an hour had passed and she was no doubt as tired of having a stranger sitting in her office as Louise was tired of waiting.

Her reason for wanting to see Dimitri was too personal and too important to discuss with anyone but him, but it suddenly occurred to Louise that on Eirenne she had been known as Loulou—the nickname her mother always called her by. And because she had a different surname from Tina maybe Dimitri did not realise her identity.

His PA looked mystified as she double-checked the new message Louise asked her to give to her boss, but she duly disappeared into his office.

The aroma of freshly brewed coffee assailed Dimitri's senses and told him without him having to check the platinum Rolex on his wrist that it was 3:00 p.m. His PA served him coffee at exactly the same time every afternoon. Aletha had been with him for five years, and she ensured that his office ran with the smooth efficiency of a well-oiled machine.

'*Efkharistó.*' He did not lift his eyes from the columns of figures on his computer screen, but he was aware of her setting the tray down on his desk. Subconsciously he listened for the faint click of the door to indicate that she had left the room.

The click did not come.

'Dimitri—if I could have a word?'

Frowning at the unexpected interruption, he flicked his gaze from the financial report he was working on and glanced at his PA. 'I asked not to be disturbed,' he reminded her, impatience edging into his voice.

'Yes, I'm sorry…but the young woman who arrived earlier and asked to see you is still here.'

He shrugged. 'As I explained earlier, I don't know Louise Frobisher. I've never heard of her before, and unless she can give a reason for her visit I suggest you call Security and have her escorted from the premises.'

Aletha Pagnotis read the warning signs that the head of Kalakos Shipping was becoming irritated. Nothing was more likely to trigger Dimitri's temper than disruption to his routine. But running a billion-pound business empire must put huge demands on him, she conceded.

At thirty-three, Dimitri was one of the country's most

powerful businessmen. Even before he had taken up the reigns of Kalakos Shipping, after the death of his father, Dimitri had set up an internet company which specialised in selling designer goods to the rapidly expanding Asian market, and within only a few years he had become a self-made millionaire. His drive and determination were phenomenal, and his brilliance and ruthlessness in the boardroom legendary.

Aletha sometimes had the feeling that he was trying to prove something to his father, even though Kostas had been dead for three years. The rift between father and son had been public knowledge, and she had always thought it a pity that they had never resolved their differences.

Whatever was behind his motivation, Dimitri set himself a demanding work schedule, and paid his staff generous salaries to see to it that his life ran like clockwork. Ordinarily she would not have bothered him about a visitor who had turned up without an appointment and refused to explain why she wanted to see him. But beneath the Englishwoman Louise Frobisher's quiet determination Aletha had sensed an air of desperation, which had prompted her to ignore Dimitri's orders that he was not to be disturbed under any circumstances.

'Miss Frobisher has asked me to tell you that you knew her several years ago by her nickname—Loulou. And that she wishes to discuss Eirenne.'

Aletha was sure she had repeated the message correctly, but now the words sounded rather ridiculous, and she braced herself for an explosion of Dimitri's anger.

His eyes narrowed and he stared at her in silence for several seconds, before to her astonishment he said tersely, 'Inform her that I can spare her precisely three minutes of my time and show her in.'

* * *

It was so quiet in the PA's office that the ticking of the clock seemed to be in competition with the thud of Louise's heart. The window offered a spectacular view over the city, but the Athens skyline did not hold her attention for long. Her nerves were frayed, and the sound of a door opening made her spin round as Aletha Pagnotis reappeared.

'Mr Kalakos will see you very briefly,' the PA said calmly. She was clearly intrigued by the situation but far too professional to reveal her curiosity. 'Please come this way.'

Butterflies leapt in Louise's stomach. *If you act confident he won't be able to intimidate you*, she told herself. But the butterflies still danced, and her legs felt wobbly as she balanced on her four-inch heels and entered the lion's den.

'So, when did Loulou Hobbs become Louise Frobisher?'

Dimitri was seated behind a huge mahogany desk. He did not get to his feet when Louise walked in and his expression remained impassive, so that she had no idea what he was thinking, but he exuded an air of power and authority that she found daunting. Her brain also registered that he was utterly gorgeous, with his dark, Mediterranean colouring and sculpted features, and as she met his cool stare her heart jolted against her ribcage.

After his PA had slipped discreetly from the room Dimitri leaned back in his chair and surveyed Louise in a frank appraisal that brought a warm flush to her cheeks. She fought the urge to tug on the hem of her skirt to try and make it appear longer. It wasn't even *that* short—only an inch or so above her knees, she reminded herself. But her elegant, sophisticated outfit, yes, a little bit provocative—chosen deliberately in the hope of boosting her self-confidence—was very different from the smart but practical navy suit she wore every day to the museum.

Unlike her mother, who had been an avid attention-seeker, Louise was quite happy to blend into the background. She wasn't used to being looked at the way Dimitri was looking at her—as if she was an attractive woman and he was imagining her without any clothes on! Her face burned hotter. Of *course* he was not picturing her naked. That wasn't a glint of sexual awareness in his olive-green eyes. It was just the sunlight slanting through the blinds and reflecting in his retinas.

He had found her attractive once before, whispered a voice in her head. And if she was absolutely honest hadn't she chosen her outfit because she'd hoped to impress him— to show him what he had lost? Once he had told her she was beautiful. But that hadn't been real, her common sense pointed out. It had been part of the cruel game he'd been playing with her, and the memories of what had happened between them on Eirenne were best left undisturbed.

'Are you married? Is Frobisher your husband's name?'

The curt questions took her by surprise. Dimitri's face was still inscrutable but she suddenly sensed an inexplicable tension about him.

She shook her head. 'No—I'm not married. I have always been Louise Frobisher. My mother called me by that silly nickname when I was younger, but I prefer to use my real name. And I was never Hobbs. I was given my father's surname, even though Tina wasn't married to him. They split up when I was a few months old and he refused to support her or me.'

Dimitri's face hardened at the mention of her mother. 'It doesn't surprise me to hear that your father was one of a long list of Tina's lovers. You're lucky she even remembered his name.'

'You're hardly one to talk,' Louise shot back, instantly defensive.

In truth Tina had *not* been the best parent in the world.

Louise had spent much of her childhood dumped in various boarding schools, while her mother had flitted around Europe with whichever man she'd hooked up with at the time. But now Tina was ill, and it no longer mattered that as a child Louise had often felt she was a nuisance who disrupted her mother's busy social life. Even in today's world of advanced medical science the word cancer evoked a feeling of dread, and the prospect of losing her mother had made Louise realise how much she cared about her.

'From what I've seen in media reports you relish being a billionaire playboy with an endless supply of beautiful mistresses. I accept that my mother isn't perfect, but are you any better, Dimitri?'

'I don't break up marriages,' he said harshly. 'I've never stolen someone's partner or wrecked a perfectly happy relationship. It is an irrefutable fact that your mother broke my mother's heart.'

His bitter words hit Louise like bullets, and even though *she* had nothing to feel guilty about she wished for the millionth time that her mother had not had an affair with Kostas Kalakos.

'It takes two people to make a relationship,' she said quietly. 'Your father chose to leave your mother for Tina…'

'Only because she chased him relentlessly and seduced him with every trick in her no doubt extensive sexual repertoire.' Dimitri's voice dripped with contempt. 'Tina Hobbs knew exactly who my father was when she "bumped into him" at a party in Monaco. It was not the chance meeting she convinced you it was. She knew Kostas would be there, and she managed to wangle an invitation to that party with the absolute intention of catching herself a rich lover.'

Dimitri's nostrils flared as he sought to control the anger that still burned inside him whenever he thought of his father's mistress. The first time he'd set eyes on Tina Hobbs he had seen her for what she was—an avaricious harlot who attached herself like a leech to any rich man stupid enough to fall for a pair of big breasts and the promise of sexual nirvana.

That was what had got to him the most. The realisation that his father hadn't been as clever or wonderful as he had believed had hurt. He'd lost respect for Kostas, who had been his idol, and even now he still felt a hard knot inside when he remembered how his illusions had been shattered.

Anger filled him with a restless energy, and he scraped back his chair and jerked to his feet. He frowned when Louise immediately edged backwards towards the door. It wasn't *her* fault that her mother was a greedy, manipulating bitch, he reminded himself. Louise had been a child when Tina had met Kostas—a gawky kid with braces on her teeth and an annoying habit of staring down at the ground as if she hoped she would sink through it and become invisible.

To tell the truth he hadn't taken much notice of her on the occasions when he had visited his father on the Kalakos family's private Aegean island and she had been staying there with her mother during the school holidays.

It had been a shock when he had gone to the island that final time—after the row with his father—and the girl he had known as Loulou had been there alone. Only she hadn't been a girl. She had been nineteen—on the brink of womanhood and innocently unaware of her allure. He'd had no idea when exactly the awkward teenager who had been too shy to say a word to him had transformed into an articulate, intelligent and beautiful adult. For the first time in his life his usual self-assurance had deserted him and he had found himself struggling to know what to say to her.

He had resolved the problem by kissing her…

Dimitri hauled his mind back to the present. Trips down memory lane were never a good idea. But as he stared at the unexpected visitor who had interrupted his tightly or-ganised work schedule, he acknowledged that in the past seven years Loulou—or Louise—had realised the potential she had shown at nineteen and developed into a stunner.

He ran his eyes over her, taking in her long honey-blond hair which was parted on one side so that it curved around her heart-shaped face and fell halfway down her back in a tumble of glossy curls. Her eyes were a deep sapphire-blue, and her red-glossed lips were a serious temptation.

Desire corkscrewed in his gut as he lowered his gaze and noted the way her fitted scarlet jacket moulded the firm thrust of her breasts and emphasised her narrow waist. Her skirt was short and her legs, sheathed in pale hose, were long and slender. Black stiletto heels added at least three inches to her height.

He trailed his eyes slowly back up her body and lin-gered on her mouth. Soft, moist lips slightly parted… He felt himself harden as an image flashed into his mind of slanting his lips over hers and kissing her as he had done many years ago.

Louise's breath seemed to be trapped in her lungs. Something was happening between her and Dimitri—some curious connection had made the atmosphere in the room almost crackle with electricity. She could not look away from him. It seemed as if an invisible force had locked her eyes with his, and as she stared at him she felt her blood pound in her ears, echoing the frantic rhythm of her heart-beat.

When she had walked into his office her first thought had been that he hadn't changed. He still held his head at that arrogant angle, as if he believed he was superior to ev-eryone else. And although he must be in his thirties now there was no hint of grey in his dark-as-ebony hair.

But of course there were differences about him. In the

seven years since she had last seen him his sleek, hand-some, could-have-been-a-model-in-an-aftershave-advert looks had grown more rugged. His face was leaner, harder, with razor-sharp cheekbones and a square jaw that warned of an implacable determination to always have his own way. The boyish air that she remembered had disappeared, and now he was a blatantly virile man at the prime of physical perfection.

Now that he was standing she was conscious of his exceptional height. He must be four or five inches over six feet tall, she estimated, and powerfully built, with the finely honed musculature of an athlete. Superbly tailored grey trousers hugged his lean hips, and at some point during the day he had discarded his tie—it was draped over the back of his chair—and undone the top buttons of his shirt to reveal a vee of darkly tanned skin and a smattering of the dark hair that she knew covered his chest.

Memories assailed her—images of a younger Dimitri, standing at the edge of the pool at the villa on Eirenne, wearing a pair of wet swim-shorts that moulded his hard thighs and left little to the imagination. Not that she had needed to imagine him naked. She had seen every inch of his glorious golden-skinned body. She had touched him, stroked him, felt the weight of him pressing her into the mattress as he lowered himself onto her…

'Why are you here?'

His abrupt question was a welcome interruption to her wayward thoughts. She released her pent-up breath on a faint sigh.

'I need to talk to you.'

'That's funny,' he said sardonically. 'I remember saying those exact words to you once, but you refused to listen to me. Why should I listen to you now?'

Louise was startled by his reference to the past. She'd

assumed that he would have forgotten the brief time they had spent together. They had been magical, golden days for her, but she had meant nothing to him—as she had later found out.

She moistened her dry lips with the tip of her tongue. 'I think you'll be interested in what I have to say. I'm putting Eirenne up for sale—and I thought you might want to buy it.'

Dimitri gave a harsh laugh. 'You mean buy back the island that belonged to my family for forty years before your mother persuaded my father on his deathbed to amend his will and leave Eirenne to her? Morally, it is not yours to sell.' He frowned. 'Nor do you have the right to sell it. Kostas named Tina as his beneficiary, and the island belongs to her.'

'Actually, I *am* the legal owner. My mother transferred the deeds into my name and I can do what I like with Eirenne—although Tina is in agreement with my decision to sell it.'

The first part of that statement at least was true, Louise thought. Her mother had been advised by her accountant to transfer ownership of the island for tax purposes. But Louise had never regarded Eirenne as hers, and her decision to sell it was a last resort to raise the huge sum of money needed to pay for Tina to have lifesaving pioneering medical treatment in the U.S. She had not discussed it with her mother, who was too ill to cope with anything more than getting through each day. Tina's chances of survival were slim, but Louise was determined she would *have* a chance.

She held Dimitri's gaze and tried not to feel intimidated by the aggression emanating from him. 'The island has been valued at three million pounds. I'm prepared to sell it to you for one million.'

His eyes narrowed. 'Why?'

She understood his surprise. The real-estate agent had clearly thought she was mad when she'd told him she was prepared to offer the small but charming Greek island set amid the turquoise waters of the Aegean Sea for considerably less than its market value.

She shrugged. 'Because I need a quick sale.'

She did not attempt to explain that she had never felt comfortable with the fact that Kostas Kalakos had left the island to her mother rather than to his family. For one thing she doubted Dimitri would believe her, and for another she did not want to bring personal feelings into what was essentially a business proposition. She needed to sell Eirenne and she was sure Dimitri would be keen to buy it. End of story.

'I know you tried to buy the island from my mother shortly after Kostas died, and she refused to sell it. Now I'm giving you the chance to own it again.'

Dimitri snorted. 'Let me guess. Tina wants you to sell Eirenne because she has spent all the money my father left her and has decided to cash in her remaining asset.'

His comment was painfully close to the truth, Louise acknowledged heavily. Since Kostas's death her mother *had* lived an extravagant lifestyle, and failed to heed warnings from the bank that her inheritance fund was running out.

'I don't intend to discuss the reason for the sale. But if you turn down my offer I will advertise Eirenne, and I've been told that it should attract a lot of interest.'

'Interest, possibly. But in case you hadn't noticed the world is in the middle of an economic recession and I doubt you'll sell quickly. Businesses in the leisure industry won't be attracted to Eirenne because it isn't big enough to be developed as a tourist destination—thankfully.'

Dimitri's words echoed what the real-estate agent had told Louise. 'Buying a private island is not a top priority for most people right now. Even billionaires are being cautious in this uncertain economic climate, and it could be months before a buyer comes forward.'

Panic coiled in her stomach. Her mother did not have months.

Dimitri studied Louise speculatively, curious when he saw the colour drain from her face. She gave the impression of self-confidence, but he sensed a vulnerability about her that reminded him of the younger woman he had known seven years ago.

She had been in her first year at university, just stepping out into the world and brimming with enthusiasm for life. Her passion for everything, especially the arts, had captivated him. Although he'd only been in his twenties, he had already been jaded by a diet of sophisticated socialites who fell into his bed with a willingness that he'd begun to find tedious. But the Loulou he had met on Eirenne that spring had been different from any other woman he'd ever known—just as she had been different from the shy teenager he'd largely ignored on the few previous occasions when he had seen her at his father's villa.

He had been intrigued by her new maturity, and they had talked for hours. Not pointless small-talk, but interesting conversations. As the days had passed he'd found that he valued her friendship and her honesty as much as he was entranced by her beauty, which was not just skin-deep but truly came from within her.

He had thought he had found something special— *someone* special. But he had been wrong.

Dimitri was conscious of a faint feeling of regret, which he immediately dismissed as he slammed the door on his memories.

'There's more to this than you're telling me,' he guessed intuitively. 'Why are you prepared to sell the island for significantly less than it's worth?'

When she did not reply he shrugged dismissively. 'Thanks for the offer, but I am no longer interested in Eirenne.' He shot her an intent look. 'It holds too many memories that I'd prefer to forget.'

Louise wondered if he deliberately meant to hurt her. He could have been referring to his father's affair with her mother, of course. Kostas had left Dimitri's mother to live with Tina on Eirenne. But somehow she knew he had been talking about more personal memories—of the few wonderful days they had spent together and that one incredible night.

He drew back his shirt-cuff and glanced at his watch. 'Your three minutes are up. A member of my security staff will escort you from the building.'

'*No*... Wait!' Shocked by his abrupt dismissal, Louise jerked forward and reached out to prevent him from picking up the phone on his desk. Her fingers touched his and the brief contact sent a quiver of electricity shooting up her arm. She could not restrain an audible gasp and snatched her hand back.

She felt his eyes on her, but she was so shaken by her reaction to him that she could not bring herself to meet his gaze. She was stunned by his refusal to buy the island. She had been sure he would agree.

Her mind whirled. If Dimitri did not want to buy Eirenne she could advertise it at the same below-value price she had offered it to him. But there was still no guarantee that it would be sold quickly, and time for Tina was running out.

She pictured her mother's painfully thin face the last time she had visited her. The slash of bright lipstick Tina still applied every day with the help of a nurse had looked garish against her grey skin.

'I'm scared, Loulou,' Tina had whispered, when Louise

had leaned over the bed to kiss her the day before she had
flown to Greece.

'It's going to be all right—I promise.'

She would do everything in her power to keep the promise she had given her mother, Louise vowed. Somehow she
had to raise enough money for Tina to have that treatment
in the U.S., and her best chance of doing that was to persuade Dimitri to buy back the island that she believed in
her heart should be his.

That was why she had offered Eirenne to him for less
than it was worth. Her conscience was torn between wanting to help her mother and a desire to be fair to Dimitri. The
figure she had quoted him would cover Tina's medical costs
at the specialist cancer clinic in Massachusetts, and would
leave enough for her to live on once she was well again.

She *had* to believe it was going to happen, Louise
thought emotionally. She refused to contemplate that Tina
would not survive. But Dimitri's declaration that he was
not interested in the island was a serious blow to her hopes.

CHAPTER TWO

'I THOUGHT you would jump at the chance to own Eirenne.' Louise prayed that Dimitri could not hear the desperation in her voice. 'I remember you told me it meant a lot to you because you'd spent happy times there as a child.'

His jaw tightened. 'They were happy times—for me, my sister and my parents. We spent every holiday on Eirenne. Until your mother destroyed my family. Now you have the gall to want me to buy back what should have been mine? My father had no right to leave our island to his whore.

'I presume you would give the money to Tina, so that she can continue to fund her extravagant lifestyle?' His lip curled in disgust. 'What kind of sucker do you take me for? Why don't you suggest she finds herself another rich lover? Or do what every other decent person does and find a job so that she can support herself? That would be a novelty,' he sneered. 'Tina actually working for a living. Although I suppose she would argue that lying flat on her back *is* a form of work.'

'*Shut up!*' The vile picture he was painting of her mother ripped Louise apart—not least because she could not deny there was some truth in his words. Tina had never worked. She had lived off her lovers and shamelessly allowed them to keep her—until a richer man came along.

But she was her mother, faults and all, and she was

dying. Louise refused to criticise Tina or allow Dimitri to insult her.

'I've told you—I am the legal owner of Eirenne and I'm selling it because I need to raise some capital.'

He frowned. 'You're saying the money would be for *you*? Why do you need a million pounds?'

'Why does anyone need money? A girl has to live, you know.'

Unconsciously she touched the diamond *fleur-de-lis* pendant and thought of her grandmother. Céline had not approved of the way her daughter lived her life, but she would have wanted her granddaughter to do everything possible to help Tina. Louise had even had the pendant valued by a jeweller, thinking that she could sell it to raise funds for Tina's treatment. But the sum she would have made was a fraction of the cost of medical expenses in America, and on the jeweller's advice she had decided to keep her only memento of her grandmother.

She flushed beneath Dimitri's hard stare. The contempt in his eyes hurt like a knife in her chest, but it was vital that she convinced him she was selling the island for her own benefit. If he guessed that Tina needed money there wasn't a hope in hell he would agree to buy Eirenne. She was not being dishonest, she assured herself. She was giving Dimitri the opportunity to buy the island that had once belonged to his family at a bargain price. It was no business of his how she chose to spend the proceeds of the sale.

'From what I remember of Eirenne it is a pleasant enough place, but I'd rather have hard cash than a lump of grey rock in the middle of the sea,' she told him.

Dimitri felt a sensation like a lead weight sinking in his stomach. It was stupid to feel disappointed because Louise had turned out like her mother, he told himself. Tina Hobbs

was the ultimate gold-digger, and it should be no surprise
that her daughter shared the same lack of moral integrity.

Seven years ago he would have sworn that Louise
was different from Tina, but clearly she was not. She
wanted easy money. From her appearance—designer
outfit and perfect hair and make-up—she was obviously
high-maintenance and had expensive tastes. Her necklace
was not some cheap trinket. Diamonds which sparkled with
such brilliance were worth a fortune.

How was she able to afford couture clothes and valuable
jewellery? Dimitri frowned as the thought slid into his head
that perhaps a man had paid for her outfit in return for her
sleeping with him. Her mother had made a career out of
leeching off rich lovers, and he was sickened to think that
Louise might be doing the same.

Seven years ago she had been so innocent, he remembered. Not sexually—although it *had* crossed his mind
when he had taken her to bed that she was not very experienced. At first she had been a little shy with him, a little
hesitant, but she had responded to him with such ardent
passion that he had dismissed the idea that he was her first
lover. Sex with her had been mind-blowing, and even now
the memory of her wrapping her slender limbs around him,
the soft cries of delight she had made when he had kissed
every inch of her body and parted her thighs to press his
mouth to her sweet feminine heart, caused his gut to clench.

Her unworldly air had probably been an act, Dimitri
thought grimly as he dragged his eyes from her face and
turned to stare out of the window. Even if she had been as
sweet and lovely as he'd believed all those years ago, she
was patently her mother's daughter now.

So why was he so fiercely attracted to her? The question mocked him, because however much he hated to admit
it he felt an overwhelming urge to stride around his desk

and pull her into his arms. He felt a tightening in his groin as he imagined kissing her, pictured himself thrusting his tongue between her red-glossed lips and sliding his hand beneath her short skirt.

Gamoto! He cursed beneath his breath. The girl Loulou he remembered from years ago had gone for ever. Perhaps she had never existed at all except for in his mind. He had made her out to be special, but he had been kidding himself.

The woman standing in his office was beautiful and desirable—and he was a red-blooded male. He wasn't going to beat himself up because she fired him up. But he was not some crass youth with a surfeit of hormones. Louise was off-limits for all sorts of reasons—not least because she was history and he had no wish to revisit the past.

Confident that he had regained control of his libido, he swung round and regarded her dispassionately. His first instinct when she had offered to sell him Eirenne had been to tell her to go to hell. But now his business brain acknowledged that he would be crazy to turn down the proposition. The island was easily worth double the amount Louise was asking. He did not know why she was prepared to sell it for less, and frankly he didn't care.

Three years ago his lawyers had contested Kostas's will and argued that Eirenne should remain the property of the Kalakos family, but to no avail. There had been no legal loopholes and Dimitri had had to accept that he would never own the island he believed was rightfully his. Now he had the chance to buy it at an exceptionally good price. He would be a fool to allow his pride to stand in the way of a good deal.

'I need some time to consider whether or not I want to buy Eirenne,' he said abruptly.

Louise hardly dared to breathe, afraid she had misheard him or misunderstood, and that the fragile thread of hope he seemed to be offering would be snatched away. A few moments ago he had told her he was not interested, but now, miraculously, he appeared to be having second thoughts.

'How much time?' She did not want to push him, but Tina needed to start the treatment in America as soon as possible.

'Three days. I'll contact you at your hotel. Where are you staying?'

'I'm not—I arrived in Greece yesterday evening and I'm leaving tonight. I can't be away from home for too long.'

Why not? Dimitri wondered. Did she live with a lover who demanded her presence in his bed every night? Was he the same man who had bought her the diamond pendant that sparkled so brilliantly against her creamy skin? Heat surged inside him—an inexplicable feeling of rage that boiled in his blood. It was none of his business how Louise lived her life, he reminded himself. He didn't give a damn if she had an army of lovers.

'Give me details of where I can contact you,' he instructed her tersely, handing her the notepad and pen from his desk.

She quickly wrote something down and handed the pad back to him. He glanced at her address and felt another flare of anger. Property in the centre of Paris was expensive. He knew because a couple of years ago he had purchased an apartment block on the *Rue de Rivoli* to add to his real-estate portfolio.

She could have a well-paid job, his mind pointed out. He shouldn't leap to the assumption that she allowed a man to keep her just because her mother had always done so. But she had told him she was selling Eirenne because she needed the money. So, had a rich lover grown tired of her? She would have to have a damn good job to afford the rent on a prime city-centre address so close to the Champs-Élysées.

Incensed by the thoughts ricocheting around his brain—about a woman he had not the slightest interest in—Dimitri strode across the room and pulled open the door for her to leave.

'I'll be in touch.'

Louise's eyes flew to his face, but she could read nothing in his hard expression. Patently their meeting was at an end. The next three days were going to seem an eternity, but she could do nothing now except wait for Dimitri's decision.

'Thank you.' Her voice sounded rusty and her legs felt as unsteady as a newborn foal's as she walked out of his office. As she passed him, she caught the drift of his cologne, mingled with another subtly masculine scent that was achingly familiar even after all this time. She hesitated, swamped by a crazy urge to slide her arms around his waist, to rest her head against his chest and feel the beat of his heart next to her own as she had done a long time ago.

Of their own volition, it seemed, her eyes were drawn to his face, and just as when she had first entered his office some unseen force seemed to weld her gaze to his. Unconsciously she moistened her lips with the tip of her tongue.

Dimitri's eyes narrowed. *Theos*, she was a temptress—and he was a mere mortal with a healthy sex drive. Despite his determination to ignore the smouldering chemistry between him and Louise he was conscious of an ache low in his gut, and his mouth twisted in self-disgust when he felt himself harden.

For the space of a heartbeat he almost gave in to the temptation to pull her back into the room, close the door and push her against it, so that he could grind the swollen shaft throbbing painfully beneath his trousers against her pelvis. It was a long time since he had felt such an urgent, almost primitive desire for a woman. He prided himself on the fact that he was always in control, always coolly collected. But he did not feel cool now. Molten heat was surging through his veins, and as he stared into her sapphire-blue eyes every sensible thought in his head was overruled by a sexual hunger that was so strong it took all his considerable will-power not to succumb to it.

'Antio.' He bade her goodbye in a clipped tone, his teeth gritted.

The sound of Dimitri's voice shattered the spell. Louise tore her eyes from his. She discovered that she had been holding her breath and released it on a shaky sigh. She forced her feet to continue moving, and the instant she stepped into the corridor she heard the decisive snick of the door being closed behind her.

For a few seconds she leaned against the corridor wall and dragged oxygen into her lungs, conscious of her heart hammering beneath her ribs. She was shocked by the effect Dimitri had had on her. He was just a man, she reminded herself. Sure, he was good-looking, but she had met other handsome men and hadn't felt as if she had been hit in the solar plexus.

She had never met another man as devastatingly sexy as Dimitri, a voice in her head taunted. No other man had ever turned her legs to jelly and evoked shockingly erotic images in her mind that caused her cheeks to burn as she hurried into the lift. Seven years ago she had been utterly overwhelmed by Dimitri, and she was dismayed to realise that nothing had changed.

Dimitri walked back across to his desk and drummed his fingers on the polished wooden surface. He could not forget the expression of relief that had flared in Louise's eyes when he had told her he would consider buying the island. Maybe she had debts and that was why she needed money in a hurry, he brooded. That would explain why she couldn't wait for a buyer who would pay the full value of Eirenne.

He dropped into his chair and stared at his computer screen, but his concentration was shot to pieces and his mood was filthy. Sexual frustration was *not* conducive to work productivity, he discovered. With a savage curse he gave up on the financial report, snatched up his phone and put a call through to a private investigator whose services he used occasionally.

'I want you to check out a woman called Louise Frobisher—I have an address in Paris for her. The usual information. Where she works—' *if* she works, he thought to himself '—her friends…' his jaw hardened '…boyfriends. Report back to me in twenty-four hours.'

It was past midnight when Louise arrived back at her apartment in the Châtelet-Les-Halles area of Paris. Ideally located close enough to the Musée du Louvre that she could walk to work, it had been her home for the past four years, and she let out a heartfelt sigh as she walked through the front door. Her flat was on the sixth floor, in the eaves of the building. The sloping ceilings made the compact interior seem even smaller, but the view over the city from the tiny balcony was wonderful.

The view was the last thing on her mind, however, as she dumped her suitcase in the hall and kicked off her shoes. The past forty-eight hours—in which she had flown to Athens and back again, and had that tense meeting with Dimitri—had been tiring, not to mention fraught with emotions.

As she entered the living room Madeleine, her Siamese

cat, stretched elegantly before springing down from a cushion on the wide windowsill.

'Don't give me that look,' Louise murmured as she lifted the cat into her arms and Madeleine fixed her with a reproachful stare from slanting eyes the colour of lapis-lazuli. 'You weren't abandoned. Benoit promised he would feed you twice a day, and I bet he made a fuss of you.'

Her neighbour, who lived in the flat below, had been a great help recently, offering to feed Madeleine while Louise spent time with Tina at the hospital. She would visit her mother after work tomorrow. For now, she knew she should eat something, but her appetite was as depleted as the interior of her fridge. A quick shower followed by bed beckoned, and half an hour later she slid between crisp white sheets and did not bother to make even a token protest when Madeleine sprang up onto the counterpane and curled up in the crook of her knees.

Sleep should have come quickly, but it eluded her as thoughts chased round inside her head. Seeing Dimitri again had been so much more painful than she had been prepared for. It had been seven years, she reminded herself angrily. She should be over him by now—*was* over him. And what was there to be over, anyway? The brief time they had spent together had hardly constituted a relationship.

But as she lay in bed, watching silver moonbeams slant through the gap in the curtains, she could not hold back her memories.

She had gone to Eirenne for the Easter holidays. Her friends at university had tried to persuade her to stay in Sheffield, but she'd had exams coming up and had guessed she wouldn't get any studying done if her flatmates planned to hold parties every night. Besides, she had planned to spend her nineteenth birthday with her mother.

But when she had arrived at the island she'd found Tina

and Kostas about to leave for a holiday in Dubai. It wasn't the first time Tina had forgotten her birthday, and Louise hadn't bothered to remind her. All her life she had taken second place to her mother's lovers. At least she would be able to get her assignment finished, she'd consoled herself. But she had been lonely on Eirenne with only the villa's staff for company, and she had missed her new university friends.

One afternoon, bored with her studies, she had decided to ride around the island on her pushbike. Eirenne was a small island, but on previous visits she had never strayed far from the grounds of the opulent villa that Kostas had built for his mistress.

The road that ran around the island was little more than a bumpy track and Louise had been carefully avoiding the potholes when a motorbike had suddenly shot round the bend and swerved to avoid hitting her. In panic she had lost her balance and fallen, scraping her arm on the rough ground as she landed.

'*Theos*, why weren't you looking where you were going?'

She had recognised the angry voice, even though she had only met Kostas's son Dimitri a handful of times when he had happened to visit his father at the same time as she had been staying on Eirenne. She had never really spoken to him before, although she had overheard the arguments he'd had with Kostas about his relationship with Tina.

'You nearly crashed into me,' she'd defended herself, her temper rising when he grabbed her arm none too gently and hauled her to her feet. 'Road hog! Some birthday this is turning out to be,' she had added grumpily. 'I wish I'd stayed in England.'

For a moment his unusual olive-green eyes darkened. But then he threw back his head and laughed.

'So you *do* speak? You've always seemed to be struck dumb whenever I've met you.'

'I suppose you think I'm over-awed by you,' she said, flushing. Not for the world would she allow him to know that since she was sixteen she'd had a massive crush on him.

He stared down at her, his eyes glinting with amusement in his handsome face. 'And *are* you over-awed, Loulou?'

'Of course not. I'm annoyed. My bike's got a puncture, thanks to you. And I'm going to have a lovely bruise on my shoulder.'

'You're bleeding,' he said, noticing where she had scraped her arm. 'Come back to the house and I'll clean that graze and fix your tyre.'

'But the Villa Aphrodite is that way,' she said in a puzzled voice when he turned in the opposite direction. 'Where are you staying, anyway? I haven't seen you around. I thought Kostas had banned you from the villa after your last row with him.'

'It suits me never to set foot inside that tasteless monstrosity my father has built for his tart.' The anger returned to Dimitri's voice. 'I'm staying at the old house my grandfather built many years ago. He named the house Iremia, which means tranquillity. But the island is no longer a tranquil place since your mother came here.'

Leaving his motorbike by the side of the track, he pushed Louise's bicycle. She followed him in silence, daunted by the rigid set of his shoulders. But his temper had cooled by the time they arrived at the house, and he was a polite host, inviting her in and instructing his butler to serve them drinks on the terrace.

The house was nestled in a dip in the land, surrounded by pine trees and olive groves so that it was hidden from view. It was not surprising that Louise had never seen it before. Unlike the ultra-modern and to Louise's mind unattractive Villa Aphrodite, Iremia was a beautiful old house built in a classical style, with coral-pink walls and cream-coloured wooden shutters at the windows. The gardens were well-established, and through the trees the cobalt-blue sea sparkled in the distance.

'Hold still while I put some antiseptic on your arm,' Dimitri instructed after he had led her out to the terrace and indicated that she should sit on one of the sun-loungers.

His touch was light, yet a tiny tremor ran through Louise at the feel of his hands on her skin. His dark head was bent close to hers, and she was fiercely aware of the tang of his aftershave mingled with another subtly masculine scent that caused her heart to race.

He glanced up and met her gaze. 'I hardly recognised you,' he said, his smile doing strange things to her insides. 'The last time I saw you, you were the proverbial ugly duckling.'

'Thanks,' she muttered sarcastically, flushing as she remembered the thick braces she'd worn on her teeth for years. Thankfully she'd had them removed now, and her teeth were perfectly straight and white.

As a teenager she had been slow to develop, and had despaired about her boyish figure, but in the last year or so she had finally gained the womanly curves she had longed for. However, she still lacked self-confidence, and Dimitri's comment hurt. She tried to jerk away from him, but instead of releasing her arm he trailed his fingers very lightly up to the base of her throat and found the pulse that was beating frantically there.

'But now you have turned into a swan,' he said softly. '*Ise panemorfi*—you are very beautiful,' he translated, although he had no need. She spoke Greek fluently.

That had been the start of it, Louise thought, turning her head restlessly on the pillows. That moment when she had looked into Dimitri's olive-green eyes and made the startling discovery that he desired her. That had been the beginning of a golden few days when they had become friends, while the awareness between them had grown ever more intense.

When Dimitri had learned that she was spending her birthday alone he had insisted on taking her to dinner on the neighbouring island of Andros, which was a short boat ride away from Eirenne. It had been a magical evening, and at the end of it, when he had escorted her back to the Villa Aphrodite, he had kissed her. It had only been a brief kiss, no more than a gossamer-light brush of his lips on hers, but fireworks had exploded inside her and she had stared at him dazedly, her heart thumping, longing for him to kiss her again.

He hadn't, but had bade her goodnight rather abruptly, so that she had wondered if she had annoyed him in some way. Maybe he regretted kissing her because she was the daughter of his father's mistress? she had thought miserably. But the next morning he had arrived as she was sitting disconsolately by the pool, facing another day on her own. He had invited her to go to the beach with him, and the day that had seemed so bleak suddenly became wonderful.

They had swum and sunbathed and talked about every subject under the sun—apart from her mother's affair with his father. Dimitri never mentioned Tina.

Over the next few days Louise's faint wariness had faded and she'd grown more relaxed with him, so that when he'd kissed her again—properly this time—she had responded with an eagerness that had made him groan and accuse her of being a sorceress who had surely cast a spell on him.

It had seemed entirely natural for him to take her back to the house in the pine forest and make love to her one long, lazy afternoon, with the sun slanting through the blinds and gilding their naked bodies. He had been so skilled and so gentle that losing her virginity had been a painless experience.

Dimitri had been unaware that it was her first time, and she had been too shy to tell him. She had responded to the stroke of his hands and the exquisite sensation of his mouth on her breasts, teasing her nipples until they were as hard as pebbles, with a passion that had matched his. It had been perfect, their bodies moving in total accord, until simultaneously they had reached the zenith of sensual pleasure.

She had spent the whole of that night with him, and each time he'd made love to her she had fallen deeper in love with him.

The following morning he had walked her back to the Villa Aphrodite.

'Come and swim in the pool,' she had invited. 'No one is here.' By 'no one' she had meant her mother.

Dimitri hesitated. 'All right—but afterwards we'll go back to Iremia. I hate this place. I assume Tina chose the décor,' he said sardonically, glancing at the zebra-print sofas and the white marble pillars that were everywhere in the villa. 'It just goes to prove that no amount of money can buy good taste.'

His dislike of her mother was evident in his voice, and Louise felt uncomfortable, but then he smiled at her and the awkward moment passed. They swam for a while, and then he carried her out of the pool and laid her on a sunbed. She had wound her arms around his neck to pull him down on top of her—when a shrill voice made them spring apart.

'What do you think you're bloody well doing? Take your hands off my daughter!'

All these years later Louise could still hear Tina screaming at Dimitri as she tottered across the patio in her vertiginous heels, quivering with fury so that her platinum-blond beehive had seemed to wobble precariously on top of her head.

'It's bad enough that Kostas cut our trip short with some excuse about needing to be at a meeting in Athens. But to find *you* here, preying on Loulou, is the last straw. You have no right to be here. Your father banned you from the villa.'

'Don't you *dare* talk to me about rights.' Dimitri's anger had been explosive as he'd leapt to his feet and faced Tina.

The row that had followed had been a vicious exchange of words. Louise had said nothing, but her mother had said more than enough.

'Do you think I don't know what's in your nasty, vengeful mind?' Tina hissed to Dimitri. 'It's obvious you decided to try and seduce Loulou to get at me—out of some misplaced revenge for your mother.'

'No!' Louise interrupted desperately. 'This has nothing to do with you.'

'Doesn't it?' Tina laughed mockingly. 'So Dimitri has *told* you about his mother, has he? That she took an overdose and that he blames me for her death? Has he also told you that his father has disinherited him because of the way he has repeatedly insulted me?' Tina continued relentlessly. 'Or that now he is no longer in line to inherit a fortune the woman he hoped to marry has dumped him? This has *everything* to do with me—doesn't it, Dimitri? You hate my guts, and the only reason you've been sniffing around my daughter is because you want to cause trouble.'

Tina's accusations sent a cold chill down Louise's spine. Her mother had always been over-dramatic, she reminded herself. Dimitri couldn't have been pretending to be attracted to her. He had been so attentive, and the passion between them had been so intense that she had even begun to think—to hope—that he was falling in love with her.

'It's not true. *Is it?*' She turned to Dimitri, pleading for his reassurance, but inside her head doubts were already forming. She had not even known his mother had died, let alone the tragic circumstances of her death. Not once in the past few days had he mentioned it.

She had thought they were friends, and now they were lovers. But Dimitri had turned into a hard-faced stranger and the coldness in his eyes froze her blood.

'*Yes, it's true.*'

His harsh voice broke the silence, and like a pebble hitting the surface of a pool his words caused shockwaves to ripple through the tense atmosphere.

'My mother took her own life because she was heartbroken that my father had divorced her and thrown away the love they had shared for thirty years for a worthless whore.'

He stared contemptuously at Tina, and then turned and walked away without saying another word. He didn't even glance at Louise; it was as if she did not exist. And she watched him go, paralysed with shock and feeling sick with humiliation that she had been nothing more to him than a pawn in his battle with her mother.

'Don't tell me you were falling for him?' her mother said, when she caught sight of Louise's stricken face. 'For God's sake, Lou, until recently he was engaged to Rochelle Fitzpatrick—that stunning American model who is regularly on the covers of the top fashion magazines. He wasn't really interested in you. Like I said, he just wants to cause trouble. A while ago Dimitri overheard me telling Kostas how keen I am for you have a good career,' Tina continued. 'He knew I would be upset if you dropped out of university to have an affair with him. I imagine he thought that if you fell for his flattery he would be able to turn you against me. And of course his ultimate goal was to cause friction between me and his father.'

Tina prattled on relentlessly, unaware of the agonised

expression in Louise's eyes. 'It's lucky I came back before he persuaded you into bed. The villa staff told me he's only been hanging around for a couple of days. Go back to university and forget about Dimitri.' She gave Louise a sudden intent look. 'You're clever. You can make something of your life. You don't need to rely on any man. And if you take my advice you'll never fall in love like I did with your father. I swore after him that I'd never let myself care about any man ever again.'

Shaken by Tina's reference to her father, whom she had never known, and traumatised by the scene with Dimitri, Louise left Eirenne within the hour. She hadn't expected to see him again, but as she climbed into the motor launch that would take her to Athens she was shocked to see him striding along the jetty.

'*Loulou*…wait!'

Wearing bleached jeans and a black tee shirt that accentuated his incredible physique, he looked unbelievably gorgeous, and it struck her then that she'd been mad to believe he could have been attracted to her. He could have any woman he wanted, so why would he want an unsophisticated student whose looks could at best be described as passable?

Overwhelmed by self-doubt, she instructed the boatman to start the engine.

Dimitri broke into a run. '*Theos!* Don't go. I want to talk to you about what I said up at the villa.'

'But I don't want to talk to *you*,' she told him stonily. 'You made everything perfectly clear.'

She felt a fool, but she'd be damned if she would let him see that he had broken her heart. The boat engine roared, drowning out Dimitri's response. He looked furious as the boat shot away from the jetty, and shouted something after her. But she didn't hear his words over the rush of the wind, and told herself she did not care that she would never speak to him again.

She had been unaware when she had left Eirenne that a few weeks later she would urgently need to talk to Dimitri...

Louise tossed restlessly beneath the sheets. She sat up to thump her pillows and flopped back down again, wishing the bombardment of memories would stop. Tiredness swept over her, and her last conscious thought was that in a few short hours she had to get up for work.

She must have fallen into a deep sleep at first, but towards dawn the dream came. She was running down a long corridor. On either side were rooms like hospital rooms, and in each room was a baby lying in a cot. But it was never her baby. Every time she went into a room she felt hopeful that this was the right one—but it was always someone else's child looking up at her.

She ran into the next room, and the next, feeling ever more frantic as she searched for her baby. She was almost at the end of the corridor. There was only one room left. This had to be where her child was. But the cot was empty—and the terrible truth dawned that she would never find her baby. Her child was lost for ever.

Dear God. Louise jerked upright, breathing hard as if she had run a marathon. It was a long time since she had last had the dream, but it had been so real she was not surprised to find her face was wet and that she had been crying in her sleep. For months after the miscarriage that she'd suffered, three weeks after discovering she was expecting Dimitri's child, she had dreamed that she was looking for her baby. And each time she had woken, just as now, feeling a dull ache of grief for the new life she had carried so briefly inside her.

Seeing Dimitri again yesterday had triggered memories buried deep in her subconscious. She had never told anyone about the baby, and had struggled to deal with her sense of loss alone. Maybe if she had been able to confide in someone it would have helped, but her mother had been totally absorbed in her relationship with Kostas, and as for Dimitri—well, it was probably better that he had never known she had conceived his child.

No doubt he would have been horrified. But she would never know how he might have reacted, because he had refused to speak to her when she had plucked up the courage and phoned him to tell him she was pregnant. A week later, when he had finally returned her call, she had switched off her phone. There hadn't seemed any point in telling him she had lost his baby. At the time there hadn't seemed a lot of point in anything. The weeks and months following the miscarriage had been desperately bleak, and she had just wanted to stay in bed and hide from the world, she remembered.

She had told herself it would not have been ideal to bring a fatherless child into the world. She knew only too well what it was like to grow up with only one parent, to feel the nagging sense of failure that perhaps it was her fault her own father had rejected her. She had tried to convince herself it was for the best that her pregnancy had ended. Yet even now, whenever she saw a child of about six years old, she imagined what *her* child would have been like and wished she could have known him or her.

Tears filled her eyes and she blinked them away. There was no point in dwelling on the past. She stroked Madeleine's downy-soft, cream fur. 'At least I've got you,' she murmured to the cat. And Madeleine, who seemed to possess an intuition that was beyond human understanding, gently purred and rubbed her pointed chocolate-coloured ears against Louise's hand.

CHAPTER THREE

'ON THIS tour of the Louvre you will be able to admire some of the world's greatest masterpieces, including the *Wedding Feast at Cana*, the *Venus de Milo*, and of course, the *Mona Lisa*.'

Louise addressed the group of visitors who were assembled in the Hall Napoléon, beneath the spectacular glass pyramid. One of her duties as a visitors' assistant was to give tours in both French, which she spoke fluently, and English. Her group this afternoon seemed to be mainly American and Japanese tourists, who nodded and smiled to show that they had understood her.

'If you would like to follow me, we will go first to the Denon Wing.'

Out of the corner of her eye she caught sight of a figure striding across the hall and she waited, assuming the man wanted to join the tour. But as he drew closer her heart performed a somersault beneath her ribs.

What was Dimitri doing here? Yesterday had been the third day since she had visited him at his office in Athens. By midnight, when he hadn't contacted her, she had assumed he had decided not to buy Eirenne, and she had spent all night worrying about how she was going to raise the money for her mother's treatment.

The rest of her tour group were already climbing the

stairs when he halted in front of her. The glint of amusement in his olive-green eyes told her he knew she was shocked to see him, and to her irritation she felt herself blush as if she was still the schoolgirl who years ago had had a huge crush on him. She hated the effect he had on her, but good manners forced her to greet him with a cool smile.

'Did you want to see me? I'm just about to conduct a tour of the museum, so I'm afraid I can't talk to you right now, but if you give me your phone number I'll call you as soon as I'm free.'

'Don't let me interrupt you.' He indicated that she should follow her tour group, and fell into step beside her as she headed towards the stairs.

'So you realised your dream,' he murmured.

She gave him a startled glance—and immediately wished she hadn't made eye contact with him when her heart gave a jolt. He was even more gorgeous in real life than in the image of him that she had been unable to dismiss from her mind for the past three days. She was supremely conscious of his height and his toned, muscular body as he walked beside her. He was wearing a suit but no tie, and the top couple of his shirt buttons were undone to reveal the tanned column of his throat. The dark stubble shading his jaw added to his raffish sex appeal.

Louise choked back a slightly hysterical laugh as she imagined his reaction if she gave in to the crazy urge to reach up and press her lips to the sensual curve of mouth. She bit her lower lip and the sharp pain brought her to her senses. 'I don't understand what you mean,' she said shortly.

'I remember you studied the history of art at university, and you told me your ambition was to work at an art museum. I think you spent some time as volunteer at the National Gallery in London while you were a student.'

'I'm sure I bored you to death, talking about my career plans.'

She was embarrassed to remember how unsophisticated she had been at nineteen. No one had ever taken much interest in her before—her mother had always been too busy with her own life. She had been dazzled by Dimitri, and had lapped up his attention like a puppy desperate to please its master, she thought painfully. It was a surprise to hear that he had actually listened to her.

'I assure you—you never bored me, Loulou,' he said softly.

His use of her nickname took her back in time—to seven years ago when she had been young and heartbreakingly naïve. She remembered the old house among the pine trees on Eirenne, the feel of warm sunshine on her skin, and Dimitri whispering her name reassuringly as he drew her down onto a bed and slanted his lips over hers. *I want you, my lovely Loulou.*

She snapped back to the present. 'Please don't call me that. I prefer to use my proper name rather than a childish nickname.'

'Louise is certainly more elegant,' he agreed. 'It suits you.'

Dimitri turned his head and subjected her to an unhurried appraisal, taking in her honey-blond hair swept up into a chignon and the functional navy-blue uniform that all the Louvre's visitors' assistants wore. She looked neat, almost demure, with barely any make-up other than a slick of pale pink gloss on her lips. Unlike when she had visited him in Athens, she was not dressed as a *femme fatale* today, but her plain clothes could not disguise her innate sensuality. Desire uncoiled in Dimitri's gut and he had to fight the urge to pull her into his arms and kiss her temptingly soft mouth.

Flustered by the hard glitter in Dimitri's eyes, Louise tore her gaze from him and increased the speed she was walking at so that she could catch up with the group of visitors ahead of her.

'Well, anyway, after I gained my degree I did a post-grad in Museum Studies, which included a three month placement at the Louvre, and I was lucky enough to be offered a permanent position.' She frowned as a thought occurred to her. 'How did you know I work here? I'm sure I didn't mention it.'

'I had a private investigator check you out.'

'You did *what*?' She stopped dead and glared at him. *'How dare you?'*

'Quite easily,' he said with a shrug. 'I needed to be sure you are the legal owner of Eirenne and that you have the right to sell it.'

It was a reasonable explanation, Louise acknowledged grudgingly. But the idea that an investigator had been nosing around in her private life was horrible, and it made her feel like a criminal. Another thought struck her. What if his sleuth had found out about her mother's illness and learned that Tina's only chance of survival was to have expensive specialist treatment in America? Had Dimitri discovered why she needed a lot of money as quickly as she could lay her hands on it?

She focused on what he had said a moment ago and looked at him uncertainly. 'When I didn't hear from you yesterday I assumed you had decided not to buy Eirenne.'

'I haven't made a decision yet. I require a little more time to think about it.'

'Oh…' Louise's breath left her in a whoosh as relief flooded through her.

Dimitri was clearly interested in buying the island— otherwise he would have told her straight that they did not have a deal. The lifeline for her mother which last night had seemed out of reach was still a possibility. She sagged against the wall, struggling to regain her composure, and did not see the intent look he gave her.

'It infuriates me that the only way I can regain ownership of my birthright, which should *never* have passed out of the Kalakos family's possession, is to buy it back,' he told her harshly. 'But my grandparents are buried on Eirenne, and my sister is distressed at the prospect of losing it for good. It is for Ianthe's sake more than anything else that I am still considering your offer, but I need more information regarding the sale. We'll discuss the details over dinner tonight.'

He hadn't lost any of his arrogance, Louise thought ruefully. It clearly hadn't occurred to him that she might not be free tonight. But he was calling the shots. If he had asked her to meet him on the moon at midnight she would have done her best to get there, because he had given her hope that her mother might have a chance of beating the disease that was ravaging her body.

They had reached the Pre-Classical Greek Gallery, where ancient sculptures were displayed on marble plinths. At the far end of the gallery, at the top of a wide staircase, stood the majestic *Winged Victory of Samothrace*. The group of visitors had paused and were waiting expectantly for Louise to begin the tour.

She glanced at Dimitri. 'I don't finish my shift until seven-thirty tonight.'

'I'll meet you at eight-fifteen at La Marianne on the Rue de Grenelle. Do you know it?'

Louise had heard of the exclusive restaurant, which had a reputation for serving the finest French cuisine and charging exorbitant prices. It was not the sort of place her salary would stretch to, she thought ruefully.

'I'll be there,' she confirmed. 'Now, I'm afraid you'll have to excuse me.'

She turned and walked away from him, fighting an uncharacteristic urge to burst into tears. She rarely cried. Ever since the miscarriage few things had seemed important enough to cry about. But her emotions seemed to be all over the place. Meeting Dimitri again had brought back painful memories.

She wished she did not have to see him again. But perhaps tonight he would agree to buy Eirenne. The sale would be dealt with by their respective lawyers, Dimitri would return to Greece, and maybe, if she tried hard enough, she would forget him, she told herself. But the assurance rang as hollow as her footsteps on the floor of the gallery.

Pinning a smile on her face, she joined her group of visitors and began the guided tour, leading them first to view the paintings in the Grande Galerie. Usually she enjoyed giving tours, but to her dismay Dimitri had joined the group, instead of leaving the museum as she had expected him to do. He made no attempt to talk to her, and appeared to listen intently to the information she gave on various artworks. She tried to ignore him and concentrate on the tour, but she found his presence disconcerting—especially when she glanced at him a couple of times and discovered his olive-green eyes were focused on *her* rather than a Raphael or a Caravaggio hanging on the gallery walls.

From the Grande Galerie she led the group into the Salle des Etats, where the *Mona Lisa*'s enigmatic expression was protected behind bulletproof glass. The world's most famous portrait needed little introduction, and Louise stood back while the visitors crowded around the barrier.

'I have to say the most famous painting in the world is rather smaller than I'd imagined,' Dimitri murmured wryly.

She tensed when she found him standing next to her, but

she could not refrain from smiling. 'I can't tell you how many times I've been told that. I hope you're not disappointed. The *Mona Lisa* is exquisite. But personally I find the *Wedding Feast at Cana* more interesting.' She turned towards the immense painting on the opposite wall. 'The colours are so intense that the figures seem to almost leap from the canvas.'

'You love your work, don't you? I can hear the passion in your voice.'

Something in Dimitri's tone caused Louise's heart to skip a beat. Passion was such an evocative word. It brought back memories of the wildfire passion they had shared on Eirenne—memories she had never been able to forget and which now flooded her mind with such shocking clarity that once again she felt herself blush. She darted him a glance, startled to find that his eyes were focused on her, and she felt certain that he was also remembering the past.

'I feel very privileged to work at the Louvre,' she admitted, thankful that she sounded cool and composed even though she did not feel it. 'But I'm surprised you decided to join the tour. Are you interested in art?'

He shrugged. 'It's not a subject I have ever studied in great detail, but even for a layman it is impossible not to be awed by the beauty and the history of the masterpieces on display. I enjoyed the tour. You have a way of bringing the works of the Great Masters to life with your expertise and enthusiasm.'

Louise's melodious voice and her impressive knowledge of the historical artworks housed in the Louvre *had* made the tour fascinating, but if Dimitri was honest he had spent more time studying the attractive guide than the paintings. She was seriously beautiful, and he was slightly ashamed of his erotic fantasy in which he ripped off her prim skirt and blouse and had hot, hungry sex with her on one of the plush red velvet bench-seats that were dotted around the gallery.

He didn't even understand what he was doing here, he thought irritably. He was interested in buying the island, but in truth he was intrigued by Louise. Seeing her again had awoken memories of the brief time they had spent together, and he had come to Paris and spent the past hour looking at paintings of fat cherubs when he should be working on the Russian deal.

He hadn't been able to get her out of his thoughts since she had turned up at his office. He had never forgotten what had happened between them on Eirenne. But seven years was a long time. During those years he had been focused on establishing his own company and then proving that he was a worthy successor to his father at Kalakos Shipping, and his memories of the pretty nineteen-year-old girl he had known as Loulou had faded.

The grown-up Louise was an attractive woman no red-blooded male would forget in a hurry, Dimitri mused. But since he was a young man he'd had more beautiful mistresses than he cared to remember. He couldn't explain what it was about Louise. All he knew was that his trousers felt uncomfortably tight, and he did not dare to meet her cool gaze in case she guessed he was fantasising about making love to her right here in the most famous art gallery in the world.

He cleared his throat. 'I come to Paris frequently for business, but I've never had time to visit the Louvre.' He glanced at his watch and grimaced. 'Regrettably, my free time rarely lasts for long. I'm due to hold a conference call in half an hour, and I must to go back to my hotel.'

There was a hint of weariness in his voice, and the fine lines fanning around his eyes told of someone who worked long hours and no doubt spent too much time in front of a computer screen. Louise felt an unwanted tug of sympathy for him. But perhaps he was tired for a different reason, she reminded herself sharply. He had a reputation as a playboy, and his numerous affairs were discussed with frenzied interest in the gossip columns. She was ashamed of the little stab of jealousy she felt when she pictured him making love to one of the gorgeous, glossy-haired American supermodels he seemed to favour. How Dimitri lived his life was of no interest to her, she reminded herself. Yet something intrigued her…

'I heard that your father named you as his successor to run Kalakos Shipping, despite his threat to disinherit you,' she murmured.

She wanted to ask him if he and his father had resolved their differences, but she did not dare mention the bitter argument between the two men about Kostas's affair with her mother.

Dimitri nodded. 'It was a shock, frankly. I hadn't expected it. You know of the rift between me and my father. I was determined to make it in business without his help and I set up my own company, which became extremely successful. But I sold Fine Living a year ago so that I could concentrate on Kalakos Shipping. Running it is a huge responsibility—especially at the moment, when my country is experiencing financial problems. The company employs thousands of staff and I have a duty to protect their jobs. Hence the importance of the business deal I am currently negotiating.'

'As you're so busy, why don't we forget dinner?' Louise seized the opportunity to avoid seeing him again. 'You have my phone number, and you can call me once you've reached a decision. There's no need for us to meet tonight.'

Dimitri's sudden smile transformed his hard-boned face

from serious to seriously sexy, and Louise felt a tingling sensation run through her right down to her toes.

'I disagree,' he drawled, the gleam of amusement in his eyes warning her that he had seen through her ploy to avoid meeting him. 'We haven't seen each other for seven years, and I'm looking forward to catching up. *Au revoir*, Louise—until tonight,' he murmured, before he strode out of the gallery, leaving her staring after him thinking that his words had sounded more like a threat than a promise.

It took Louise ten minutes to walk back to her flat after she had finished work. Often in the summer she liked to stroll along by the Seine and browse among the booksellers' stalls, but this evening she was in a hurry.

As soon as she arrived home she fed Madeleine and called the hospital to check on her mother, explaining to the nurse that she would visit tomorrow. Then she showered, blow-dried her hair and applied make-up in record time, aware that she was due to meet Dimitri in twenty minutes.

At least choosing something to wear was not a problem. Her friend and neighbour Benoit was a fashion designer, who regularly gave her his stunning creations, and there were several dresses in her wardrobe that she'd never had an opportunity to wear before.

One cocktail dress in particular seemed suitable for dinner at an exclusive restaurant. The simple sheath of black silk skimmed her breasts and hips and flared slightly at the hemline, which was decorated with layers of tulle ruffles. It was a striking design, and as with all Benoit's clothes very feminine and very sexy. Louise almost lost her nerve as she studied her reflection and noted how the sheer material seemed to caress her curves. The black silk felt cool and sensual against her skin, and for the first time in years she felt intensely aware of her body.

She briefly debated whether to change into something less eye-catching, but time was racing—at least that was the excuse she made to herself. The truth was that ever since she had met Dimitri in Athens she'd felt quite unlike her usual sensible self. Every time she thought of him—and he seemed to dominate her thoughts—molten heat pooled low in her pelvis and she felt an ache of sexual longing that she hadn't experienced since she was nineteen. Perhaps it was because he had been her first lover—her *only* lover, she amended ruefully. She had dated a few other men since, but none of them had caused her heart to race like Dimitri did.

What was she trying to tell him tonight by wearing this dress? That she was fiercely aware of him, and that she had glimpsed the hungry gleam in his eyes when he had met her at the Louvre? She could not answer herself, or explain the hectic flush on her cheeks. It was easier to turn away from the mirror and slide her feet into the strappy black stiletto sandals that matched the dress. A silver purse and a dove-grey pashmina completed her outfit, and she hurried out of her flat, her heart thudding.

As she stepped out of the lift on the ground floor she cannoned into a man who had just entered the apartment block.

'*Fais attention!*' His frown cleared when he recognised Louise, and he caught hold of her shoulder and studied her intently. '*Chérie*, you look divine in that dress.'

Louise smiled at Benoit Besson. 'I'm glad you approve—seeing as it's one of your creations.'

A grin flashed on Benoit's thin face and he pushed his long black hair out of his eyes. 'I can see why I am called a genius,' he drawled, only half-jokingly. 'Where are you going? Don't tell me you have a date?' He looked surprised. 'It's about time. You are too beautiful to live your life alone. You need a lover, *chérie*.'

'I'll never *need* a man,' Louise said firmly. She had vowed years ago that she would never copy her mother. Tina had always needed a man in her life, and she had lurched from one disastrous affair to the next without ever pausing to consider whether she would be happier without the jerks she hooked up with.

Kostas Kalakos had been better than most, Louise remembered. He had seemed genuinely to care for Tina. And he had been kind to *her* when she had stayed on Eirenne in the school holidays. But she could not forget that he had left his wife to pursue his affair with her mother—a fact that Dimitri had certainly never forgotten either, she thought heavily.

Benoit gave her a speculative look. 'So—not a date, but in *that* dress you can only be meeting a man. I can't deny I am curious, *mon amie.*'

'I'm having dinner with a friend I used to know years ago…an acquaintance, really.' Louise felt herself blush. 'I must go or I'll be late.'

'Have fun.' Benoit's smile was decidedly smug. 'I'm flying to Sydney in the morning, but you can tell me all about this non-date when I come back.'

Her friendship with Benoit went back many years. Benoit's grandmother had been a close friend of her *grand-mère*, Céline, and Louise had known him when he was a student—before he had taken the fashion world by storm. He was the closest she had to a brother, and she treated his teasing with affection.

'There'll be nothing to tell,' she promised him, and hurried out before he could ask any more questions.

Dimitri had chosen a seat at the bar at La Marianne, which afforded him a clear view of the door. During the past ten minutes half a dozen blondes, wearing the ubiquitous little black dresses, had entered the restaurant, and all of them had sought to make eye-contact with him—even the ones who were hanging on to the arm of a husband or boyfriend, he noted sardonically. He considered it a matter of luck that he had been blessed with facial features that women found attractive, but cynically he suspected that his huge wealth meant he could have resembled the Hunchback of Notre Dame and still have had females flocking to his bed.

He ordered a drink and glanced towards the door again. This time his attention was riveted by the blonde in a black dress who had just walked in.

Hair the colour of honey was swept into a loose knot on top of her head, and a few stray curls framed a heart-shaped face dominated by eyes that even from a few feet away he could see were sapphire-blue. She looked as though she had been poured into the black silk dress which moulded her hourglass figure as faithfully as a lover's touch, and her long legs, sheathed in barely-there black silk hose, looked even sexier with the addition of four-inch stiletto heels.

Despite his intention not to allow Louise to affect him, Dimitri felt a sharp tug of desire jack-knife through him. He lifted his glass and drained his whisky sour, but his eyes seemed determined to stray towards her.

Most women would have teamed the striking diamond *fleur-de-lis* with matching earrings, and perhaps a diamond ring or bracelet, but Louise's decision to wear only the pendant and no other jewellery gave her an understated elegance. Her dress was almost starkly plain compared to some of the exotic outfits on display in the restaurant, but clearly she understood that the beauty of haute couture was the fact that it allowed a woman to wear the dress rather than the dress wear the woman.

Dimitri recognised the designer motif of two entwined letter Bs on Louise's purse. Benoit Besson had taken the fashion world by storm after revealing his first collection at Paris Fashion Week two years ago, and had quickly become the darling of Europe's social elite. But the price of Besson's clothes reflected his undoubted skill as a designer. Louise's dress might easily have cost upwards of five or six thousand pounds, yet he knew her job as a museum guide would not pay a high salary.

Dimitri ran his mind over the facts the private investigator had dug up about her. There wasn't much, and so far no evidence of a rich lover in Louise's life. She lived alone, worked, as he knew, at the Louvre, and socialised occasionally with colleagues from the museum. But if she was not the mistress of some rich guy how could she afford to wear Benoit Besson designs? And why did she suddenly need money so quickly that she was prepared to sell Eirenne for considerably less than the island was worth? The idea that she was in debt seemed a logical possibility. Her mother's track record with money was appalling, and it was conceivable that Louise had inherited Tina's inability to live within her means.

She had hesitated when she had entered the restaurant, but now she looked towards the bar and saw him. Even though Dimitri was a few feet away from her he noticed the sudden flush of colour that highlighted her high cheekbones, and he felt a fierce sense of male satisfaction that she could not hide her awareness of him. The evening promised to be interesting, he mused, feeling suddenly more alive than he had done in months as anticipation made his nerve-endings tingle.

He stood up from the bar stool and walked over to meet her.

'Louise, you look stunning.' He bit back the question— *How the hell can you afford to wear a dress that probably cost a chunk of your annual salary?*

The bar was crowded. Someone knocked into her and Dimitri caught hold of her arm to steady her as she swayed slightly on her high heels.

Her skin felt like satin beneath his fingertips and her perfume, a delicate floral fragrance, teased his senses. Without stopping to question what he was doing, he lifted her hand to his mouth and grazed his lips over her knuckles. He heard her faint gasp and smiled when she blushed. For a moment he was reminded of the innocent girl he had known seven years ago.

But she was no longer a gauche teenager. She was a beautiful woman, and undoubtedly sexually experienced. He pictured her naked in his bed, pictured himself sinking between her thighs...

Their eyes met, held, and he watched her pupils dilate so that they were deep, dark pools. He could almost taste the intense sexual awareness between them.

It was a relief when the *maître d'* appeared and informed him that their table was ready.

Get a grip, Dimitri ordered himself impatiently, irritated that he seemed to have no control over his hormones. Louise was stunning, but no more so than countless other women he had dated in the past. And he should not forget that he was here for one reason only. He had invited her to dinner to discuss a business deal—namely the possibility of him buying back his family's Greek island, which should never have been hers to sell.

He remembered how shocked he'd felt when he had learned that his father had left Eirenne to his mistress. Dimitri hated Tina Hobbs to the depths of his soul. But he had never had cause to hate Tina's daughter, he acknowledged. In fact, far from disliking her, he had found himself captivated by her seven years ago. They had been lovers, but they had shared more than just sex. There had been something between them—a degree of emotional involvement he had not wanted to define.

Those memories had always lingered in the back of his mind, and sometimes when he heard a song that had been popular at the time he felt a curious pang inside as he remembered Eirenne in springtime and a golden-haired girl whose gentle smile had briefly touched his soul.

Startled by thoughts that he had never cared to dwell on too deeply before now, he threw Louise a sideways glance as they followed the waiter to their table—and discovered that she was looking at him with an unguarded expression that made him want to forget dinner, forget everything but his burning desire to sweep her into his arms and carry her out of the restaurant and into the nearest hotel, where he would hire a room for as many nights as it took to sate himself on her gorgeous body.

CHAPTER FOUR

THERE was champagne chilling in an ice-bucket. The white damask cloth was pristine, and the silver cutlery gleamed in the flickering light of candles set amid a centrepiece of white roses and fragrant mauve freesias. Louise tried to focus on the beautiful table setting, but in her mind all she could see was the look of scorching desire in Dimitri's eyes as he had drawn out a chair for her to sit down.

She was shaken by the sexual hunger he had made no effort to disguise. It was all the more shocking because they hadn't seen each other for seven years and were little more than strangers. She tried to block out her memories of the one night they had spent together. It had been so long ago, and he must have slept with so many other women since then that it did not seem likely he would remember. But somehow she knew that he *did* remember, and heat surged through her veins, making her breasts ache and evoking a dragging sensation low in her pelvis.

'Champagne, *mademoiselle*?'

'Oh…*oui. Merci.*' She nodded distractedly to the waiter, who was hovering at her elbow, and watched him fill a tall flute with champagne. The waiter walked around the table to fill Dimitri's glass and then presented them both with a menu before he finally left them alone.

'I think a toast to old friends is appropriate,' Dimitri murmured, raising his glass.

Friends. Louise felt a sharp pang as she remembered laughter and lazy days on a paradise island. She had thought they were friends—until her mother had shattered her illusions about Dimitri's motives. None of it had been real. Not the companionship or the friendship—or the passion. Dimitri had deliberately set out to seduce her, knowing that his actions would anger her mother, and his aim had been to cause trouble between Tina and his father. How could he have the nerve to suggest a toast to their friendship when it had been a lie? Louise wondered bleakly.

But there was no point in dragging up the past when she would probably never see him again after tonight. Somehow she managed a cool smile and touched her glass to his. 'To friends.'

Her throat felt parched and the words emerged as a husky whisper. She sounded like a *femme fatale* from an old movie, she thought disgustedly, and took a long sip of champagne to ease the dryness. The bubbles fizzed on her tongue and it belatedly occurred to her that it was hours since she'd had lunch, and alcohol on an empty stomach was not a good idea.

Focus on the reason why you're here, she told herself as she forced herself to meet his brooding gaze across the table.

'You said you might be interested in buying Eirenne. Is there any information I can give you that might help with your decision?'

Dimitri took a sip of champagne before answering. 'I haven't been back to the island for seven years, but I have many memories of it. Has it changed much?' His jaw hardened. 'Surely even your mother can't have done too much damage to the place?'

'Of course she hasn't.' Louise instantly leapt to her mother's defence. 'What do you imagine she might have done?'

'When my father was alive she tried to persuade him to build a nightclub and casino, so that she could hold private parties rather than have to travel to one of the bigger islands for entertainment,' he told her dryly.

'Oh.' Louise grimaced. Owning a nightclub was just the sort of thing Tina would have loved, she acknowledged ruefully. Her mother would not have worried about spoiling the peace and tranquillity of Eirenne.

'Well, she hasn't done anything like that. In fact she hasn't been back to the island since Kostas died.' She hesitated, and then said huskily, 'I know you believe Tina was only interested in your father because he was wealthy, but I think she really loved him.'

Dimitri shot her a sardonic look. 'The only person Tina Hobbs has ever loved is herself. *Theos*, even you must admit she was not a great mother. I know you spent most of your childhood dumped in boarding schools while she lived the high life, flitting from one rich sucker to another. My father was the biggest sucker of all, and I blame him as much as Tina for breaking my mother's heart.'

Dimitri's voice had risen, attracting curious glances from people at a nearby table. He muttered something beneath his breath and snatched up his menu, and Louise did the same, holding it in front of her so that she did not have to meet his angry gaze. Tension simmered between them. She took another gulp of champagne and welcomed the slight feeling of light-headedness as the alcohol hit her bloodstream.

The evening was on course to be a disaster, and the only surprise was how much she cared. Maybe she should leave? It was doubtful she could say anything that would persuade Dimitri to buy Eirenne. He was arrogant and powerful and it was clear he made his own decisions. There seemed little point in her staying.

She put down her menu, and a tremor ran through her when she discovered he was watching her. He didn't look angry any more, but she could not define the expression in the green eyes that glittered beneath his heavy brows.

'Louise, I'm sorry,' he said roughly. 'The last thing I want to do is drag up past issues that have nothing to do with us. My father's relationship with your mother was never our concern.'

Taken aback by his apology, she gave him a startled glance. 'How can you say that? You blame Tina...'

'My feelings about her are irrelevant,' he insisted. 'Look...' He leaned across the table, his expression intent as he held her gaze. 'I don't want to fight with you, *pedhaki mou*.'

What he wanted to do was walk around the table and pull Louise into his arms; feel her soft, curvaceous body pressed up against him as he crushed her lips beneath his, Dimitri acknowledged silently. Would she respond to him? His gut instinct told him that she was as fiercely aware of him as he was of her, and he was sure that, like him, she remembered the passionate night they had spent together seven years ago.

But there was a correct order to seduction, which he intended to follow. His body might be acting as if he was a hormone-crazed adolescent, but first they would enjoy good food and conversation, and he would savour the anticipation of bedding her as he'd savour a fine wine.

'What I would like to do,' he said softly, 'is to forget the past and pretend that we've only just met. Let us imagine that we are strangers, having dinner in Paris and getting to know one another a little better. What do you say?'

'I...'

Louise could not tear her eyes from Dimitri's face. He was as beautiful as a Michelangelo sculpture. She studied the chiselled lines of his cheekbones and his square jaw and longed to run her fingers over his five o'clock stubble, trace the sensual curve of his mouth. That gentle endearment, '*pedhaki mou*', had weakened her defences. If she had any sense she would insist that she only wanted to discuss the sale of the island, keep their conversation strictly to business and leave as soon as they had finished dinner.

Instead she heard herself say huskily, 'All right. I guess it would be nice to enjoy dinner without tension and probably indigestion.'

Her stomach had felt as if it was tied in knots since she had left her flat, but Dimitri's smile—or maybe it was the champagne—had induced a relaxed, warm feeling inside her. What harm could come from spending a pleasant evening in the charming surroundings of La Marianne?

The answer was directly in front of her, his dark head bent so close to hers that she could feel the soft whisper of his breath on her cheek. Her instincts warned her that Dimitri posed a serious threat to her peace of mind. But she was no longer an innocent nineteen-year-old. She was twenty-six, a self-confident career woman, and she would never make the mistake of falling for a man just because he had the dark, devastating looks of a fallen angel and a glint in his eyes that promised heaven.

'Good.' Dimitri sat back and noted that the hunted look in Louise's eyes had faded. For a moment, when the subject of her damned mother had come up, he had been consumed with the usual bitterness he felt towards Tina. But when he'd noticed Louise's expression he had controlled his anger and regretted that he had upset her. That had certainly not been his intention when he had invited her to dinner. He wasn't actually sure why he had arranged to meet her.

It had been a spur-of-the-moment decision—which for a man who never did anything on impulse was highly unsettling, he thought wryly.

He glanced at the extensive menu written in French and decided he needed a translator. 'Would you mind helping me choose what to eat? I can speak French reasonably well, but I'm not so good at understanding the written word.'

'Yes, of course.' Louise's heart did a little skip at his rueful smile, that made him seem more human somehow. Perhaps he wasn't as arrogant as she had first thought. She studied the menu. 'You had better not have *moules à la crème* or *coquilles Saint-Jacques.* I assume you're still allergic to shellfish?'

'I am, but I'm impressed that you remembered.'

She flushed and silently cursed herself for letting slip that she hadn't forgotten anything about him during the past seven years. 'It's surprising how many random facts linger in our brains,' she murmured. 'I read a food critic's report which recommended La Marianne's speciality—roasted beef fillet served with horseradish sauce,' she added, quickly changing the subject.

'That sounds good. I'll come closer so that you can talk me through the other main courses.'

Before she could object Dimitri had moved his chair around the table and sat down beside her, so close that his thigh pressed against hers. She stared at the menu and tried to banish the thought that if she turned her head her lips would be mere centimetres from his.

The spicy scent of his aftershave tantalised her senses and intensified her awareness of his raw masculinity. The bare skin of her arm felt acutely sensitive when she brushed against the sleeve of his jacket and, glancing down, she was mortified to see that her nipples had hardened and were jutting provocatively beneath her silk dress.

She hurriedly began to explain the menu options, but her voice emerged as that embarrassing husky whisper again, and she quickly gulped down more champagne. It was a relief when the waiter came over to take their order and Dimitri moved to back to his side of the table.

'How long have you lived in Paris?' he asked as he refilled her glass.

'Four years. But it has always seemed like home. My grandmother used to live close to Sacré-Coeur, and when I was a child I spent many school holidays with her.'

Dimitri looked puzzled. 'Was she your father's mother?'

'No, my *grand-mère*, Céline, married my grandfather, Charles Hobbs, and they lived in England, where my mother was born. But when my grandfather died she moved back to Paris.' Unconsciously, her hand strayed to the diamond *fleur-de-lis* as she thought of her beloved grandmother. In many ways Céline had been more of a mother to her than Tina, and Louise still missed her.

The first course arrived, and conversation halted while the waiters fussed around them. Glancing across the table, Dimitri frowned when he saw the faintly wistful expression on Louise's face as she touched the diamond pendant. Was she thinking of whoever had given it to her? A wealthy lover, perhaps?

He was surprised by the sudden violent urge to wrench the necklace from around her throat. Even worse was the realisation that even if she had a dozen lovers he still wanted her. Maybe it was a stupid male pride thing, but he was certain that if she spent a night with him the other man or men in her life would be history.

He ate automatically, without really being aware of what he was eating. He was sure the food was superb, but he could not concentrate on it when he was captivated by the woman sitting opposite him. Like him, Louise did not appear interested in the food, and only picked at her starter and main course. He glanced at her, and felt something coil deep in his gut when he found that she was watching him. Colour winged along her high cheekbones and she quickly dropped her gaze.

'You must know Paris well, as you've spent so much time here,' he murmured.

She nodded. 'It's a beautiful city. You said you often come here on business. Have you done much sightseeing?'

'Only of hotel conference facilities and company boardrooms,' he said wryly.

'That's a pity. You should take a coach tour, or a river cruise.'

'Maybe I'll do that. But I'd need a guide—someone who knows Paris well and is knowledgeable about its history.' He held her gaze. 'Are you interested?'

Maybe it was a trick of the candlelight, but there seemed to be a wicked glint in Dimitri's eyes, and Louise sensed that his question held a double meaning. Surely it was her over-active imagination after too much champagne? she told herself. But some invisible force seemed to have welded her gaze to his, and her heart was beating so hard that it felt as though it would burst through her ribcage.

'I expect you'll have to return to Greece soon,' she said abruptly.

'I leave Paris tomorrow. But we still have tonight.' Dimitri gave up on his *entrecôte hongroise* and reached across the table to capture her hand in his. He felt the tiny tremor that ran through her and tightened his grip a fraction to prevent her from snatching her fingers away. 'I understand the view from the top of the Eiffel Tower at night is spectacular.'

Louise was finding it hard to concentrate as Dimitri stroked his thumb over the pulse beating frantically in her

...you...you want to climb the Eiffel Tower?' she asked

...t particularly, he thought to himself, but he was reluctant for the evening to end. He had a feeling that Louise would refuse an invitation to go on to a nightclub. She seemed edgy again, although he wasn't sure why, and his instincts told him that once they had finished dinner she would bid him goodnight. He did not want to let her go. He wanted to spend more time with her, get to know her better. Okay, if he was honest he wanted to slide that tantalising slip of black silk from her body and kiss her naked breasts before trailing his lips over her stomach and lower...

He inhaled sharply and focused on persuading her to spend the remainder of the evening with him. 'I confess I was hoping to take the elevator to the top.'

Dimitri's sexy smile made Louise's pulse race. 'That would be sensible, as there are well over a thousand steps,' she said gravely. 'And actually the only way to reach the summit *is* by lift.'

'So, that's settled. But first would you like dessert—or more champagne?'

'No, thank you,' she assured him quickly. Her appetite had disappeared and she had struggled to eat the first two courses. As for champagne—she had already drunk way too much. That had to explain why she felt so peculiar. It was as if the bubbles had exploded inside her and filled her with a wild, reckless energy.

But deep down she knew it was Dimitri, not the champagne, that was making each of her nerve-endings feel ultra-sensitive. She felt fiercely alive, and was so intensely aware of him that throughout the meal she had kept darting little glances at him, drinking in his handsome features.

It was a relief when they left the restaurant and she took deep breaths of fresh air, grateful for the gentle breeze that cooled her hot face. The Eiffel Tower dominated the sky-line, its giant metal structure illuminated by light projectors so that it appeared to glow gold against the inky-black sky.

The famous landmark was a popular attraction, even late at night, and there was a short queue waiting for the elevator. The young couple standing in front of them had clearly been caught up in the romantic atmosphere of Paris and were wrapped in each other's arms.

It must be wonderful to be so in love, Louise thought wistfully. The couple's unrestrained passion reminded her of those few days on Eirenne years ago, when Dimitri had kissed her with fierce hunger and she had eagerly responded to him. Heat surged through her and she could not bring herself to look at him or at the kissing couple. In desperation she stared at the ground, as if she was utterly fascinated by the tarmac beneath her feet.

They rode the lift to the second level, and then another elevator whisked them to the top of the tower. Louise heard Dimitri catch his breath as they stepped out onto the walkway.

'I hope you have a head for heights. We're over a thousand feet up.'

He laughed. 'It feels as though we are in the sky. The view is amazing.' He stood close beside her and stared through the wire cage that enclosed the walkway. 'Is that the Arc de Triomphe down there?'

Louise nodded. 'The lights of the city sparkle like jewels, don't they? I love the way they are reflected in the river.'

The night-time view over Paris was breathtaking. But there was another reason why she was finding it difficult to draw oxygen into her lungs. The few other visitors who had come up to the top level had walked around the other side of the tower, and it felt as though it was just her and Dimitri standing on the top of the world. She had never felt so aware of a man in her life. Her eyes were drawn to his sculpted profile and a tremor ran through her, making the tiny hairs all over her body stand on end.

The breeze was stronger this high up and the air cooler. She drew her pashmina round her shoulders and caught Dimitri's attention.

'Are you cold? Do you want my jacket?'

She shook her head. 'No, I'm fine.'

'Liar,' he said softly, 'you're shivering.'

His eyes were shadowed in the darkness, but Louise could feel his intent gaze. Far below the lights of Paris blazed, but for Louise nothing existed but the sultry heat in Dimitri's eyes. All evening she had been agonisingly aware of him, and now she could no longer fight the fire surging through her veins.

'Come here.'

His voice was suddenly rough and deep, caressing her senses like crushed velvet. Her breath caught in her throat and she could not move when he slid an arm around her shoulders and pulled her against his chest. The warmth of his body immediately enfolded her and the sensual musk of his aftershave swamped her senses. She could feel the thud of his heart beating at the same frantic pace as her own and she stared up at him, her eyes wide and unguarded.

Dimitri muttered something beneath his breath. He had wanted to kiss Louise all evening, and now the temptation of her moist, slightly parted lips was too strong for him to resist. He dipped his head and slanted his mouth over hers. He remained poised for timeless seconds while their breath mingled. Then he captured her lips in a feather-soft caress, slowly at first, gently. She tasted of champagne, and the feel of her soft mouth beneath his made his heart pound.

She made a little choked sound and stiffened, but he tightened his arms around her, drawing her inexorably closer to him. Wildfire excitement shot through him when she opened her mouth so that he was able to explore her with his tongue.

Molten heat was coursing through Louise, suffusing her entire body with delicious warmth. Her breasts felt swollen and heavy and her nipples tingled as they were crushed against Dimitri's chest. She was conscious of a throbbing sensation deep in her pelvis—a restless ache that drove her to press her hips against his rock-hard thighs.

He kept on kissing her and kissing her, his mouth moving hungrily over hers, demanding a response which she gave unresistingly. *Stupid*, taunted a voice in her head, *weak and pathetic. Where is your pride?* But she ignored the voice, pushed it to the back of her mind while her body capitulated to his exquisite seduction, and she slid her hands to his shoulders as he deepened the kiss to something so erotic that she trembled in the circle of his arms.

Voices shattered the magic and snapped Louise back to her senses. People were heading towards them along the walkway. She pulled out of Dimitri's arms, breathing hard. Her mouth felt bruised, and she lifted her fingers to her lips and felt their swollen softness.

Dear heaven, what had she been *thinking*? All evening she had been haunted by memories of their brief affair years ago, but that was no excuse for her to fall into his arms. Life had moved on—*she* had moved on—and the past was history.

'You shouldn't have done that,' she whispered, dismayed to realise she was shaking from the firestorm of passion he had evoked in her.

'But you didn't stop me.' His eyes glittered, and his smile was faintly mocking, but the hand that gently brushed a tendril of hair back from her cheek shook slightly, and Louise realised with a jolt that he was no more in control of his emotions that she was.

She shivered again—a combination of reaction to his kiss and being deprived of the warmth of his body. But this time he kept his arms by his sides.

'We should go.' His voice was suddenly terse.

They were both silent as the lift whisked them back down to the ground. It was nearly midnight, Louise saw when she glanced at her watch. She was glad when Dimitri hailed a taxi. She was still stunned by that kiss, mortified when she remembered how she had responded to him. She should have given him the big freeze, hung on to her dignity. But instead she had melted in his arms as if she had spent the past seven years missing him—which she certainly had *not*, she assured herself.

They had barely discussed the sale of Eirenne, she remembered as she stared out of the taxi window. *Why* hadn't she stuck to business over dinner? And what had induced her to agree to go to the top of the Eiffel Tower with him when she knew full well that it was one of the most iconic venues in Paris, the city of lovers? The romantic atmosphere was no excuse for the fact that she had practically eaten him. She felt hot with shame when she recalled how she had clung to him.

The taxi drew to a halt and she climbed out onto the pavement after Dimitri, frowning when she realised that they were not at her apartment—which was where she had assumed they had been heading. She glanced at the grand front entrance of a well-known hotel and then at him, her eyes questioning.

He gave her a level look. 'Do you want to join me for a drink? We can continue our discussion on the possibility of me buying Eirenne.'

Persuading him to buy the island was the only thing that

mattered—the only realistic chance of saving her mother. Yet Louise knew it would be the height of stupidity to accept his invitation when he was looking at her with an intent expression in his eyes that made her blood pound in her veins.

So why didn't she bid him goodnight and climb back into the taxi? Why did her mind keep replaying his kiss? She stared at him, knowing she should refuse to join him but unable to bear the thought of leaving him. After tonight she would probably never see him again.

She shivered—but not because she was cold.

Dimitri's eyes darkened. He caught hold of her hand and lifted it to his mouth, grazing his lips across her knuckles. 'Come with me?' he murmured, in a voice as rich and sensuous as molten chocolate.

She gave up the fight with herself and nodded her assent, feeling beyond words, beyond the boundaries of common sense. Dimitri paid the taxi driver and, still holding Louise's hand, led her into the hotel. She had a vague image of an opulent lobby: elegant pillars, ornately patterned marble floor and extravagant gold décor. They entered a lift. Moments later they arrived at the top floor and walked a short distance along a corridor until he stopped and ushered her into his suite.

'What a beautiful room,' she murmured, desperate to break the silence and bring an element of normality into an increasingly unreal situation.

The suite was a luxurious blend of pale grey velvet carpet and silk wallpaper, with cushion-filled sofas and soft furnishings in duck-egg-blue. Through an open door Louise saw that the colour scheme was repeated in the bedroom, but the sight of a vast four-poster bed made her quickly look away.

'I spend too much time in hotels to appreciate them.'

Dimitri shrugged out of his jacket and dropped it over the arm of a sofa before walking over to the bar. He took two glasses, filled them, and strolled back across the room to hand one to Louise. 'A nightcap—Cointreau,' he explained.

She really did not need any more alcohol, but it seemed safer to sip the drink than to make eye-contact with Dimitri. The orange-tasting liqueur was sweet, but with a subtle heat that elicited a delicious warm feeling inside her—yet she could not seem to control the tremors that were making her body shake.

'Please—have a seat.' He indicated the two-seater sofa.

Louise stared at it and froze as she pictured herself sinking against the cushions and Dimitri sitting down close beside her. She was desperately aware of his lean, hard body, and now that he had discarded his jacket she could see the shadow of dark chest hair beneath his white silk shirt.

She shouldn't have come here, she thought frantically. She felt helpless, like a fly trapped in a spider's web. But to be fair she was not afraid of Dimitri but of herself, her reaction to his brooding sensuality.

Her glass was still half full. Not wanting to appear rude, she swallowed the rest of her drink and felt it burn a fiery path down her throat.

'Look, it's getting late. I'm not sure there's much more I can tell you about Eirenne. I haven't been back there since we…' She faltered as memories of the passionate night they had spent together on the island flooded her mind. 'Since we were there seven years ago. Perhaps you would be good enough to phone me when you have made a decision?' Panic made her talk too fast. 'Thank you for dinner. You're leaving tomorrow, so I guess we won't have a chance to meet again,' she finished in a choked voice.

She did not notice the faint flare of impatience in

Dimitri's eyes—did not know that the betraying tremor of her lower lip had made his gut clench.

'You little idiot,' he said roughly. 'Do you really think I can let you walk away from me?'

Her eyes flew to his face and she caught her breath at the hard glitter in his olive-green gaze. Time stopped. Her heart was thundering so hard that her ribcage jerked erratically. He drained his glass and set it down on the table. She waited, barely able to breathe, as he walked towards her with determined intent.

'Louise,' he said, in a low, a sexy growl that made her skin prickle. 'Come to me, *pedhaki.*'

A warning voice clamoured inside her head. But she was deafened by the thunderous beat of her heart and with a little cry went into his arms. The world exploded.

CHAPTER FIVE

THE room tilted as Dimitri seized Louise in his arms and sank down on the sofa, pulling her onto his lap. His dark head swooped and he captured her mouth in a searing kiss that destroyed any idea she might have had of resisting him. This was what she had yearned for all evening, she admitted silently. No man had ever excited her in the way Dimitri did, and she had no self-protection against the sensual onslaught of his lips and the bold thrust of his tongue into her mouth as he explored her with hungry passion.

His hands roamed feverishly over her body and traced the length of her spine, before he cupped her nape and tugged her head back so that he could deepen the kiss. It became flagrantly erotic. He moved his other hand to her shoulder, slid a finger beneath the narrow strap of her dress and drew it down her arm, lower and lower, slowly exposing her breast.

The air felt cool on her naked flesh, but Dimitri's touch was warm as he curled his hand possessively around the soft mound. Sensation arrowed through Louise as he trailed his lips down her throat and found the pulse thudding frantically at its base. The brush of his thumb-pad across her sensitised nipple made her catch her breath.

She was on fire for him. Molten heat flooded between her legs and she gave a little desperate moan when he slipped his hand beneath the hem of her dress and stroked her taut, trembling thighs. Higher and higher his fingers crept, inching towards where she was frantic for him to touch her. She was lost in a swirling sea of sensation where nothing mattered but that she follow the dictates of her body, which was begging for sexual release. Her sensible self had deserted her, and she was gripped by an urgent need for Dimitri to relieve the pressure that was building inside her.

He discovered the strip of bare flesh above the lace band of her stocking-top and made a primitive growl deep in his throat. The sound was raw and it triggered a throb of white-hot desire in Louise. And then his hand was at the junction of her thighs, and he eased the edge of her French knickers aside so that he could run his fingertips up and down her moist opening.

He eased her back so that she was half lying across his knees, with her head resting against the cushions. Glancing down, she saw the whiteness of her bare breast above the crumpled black silk of her dress. Her nipple was taut and erect, and she shivered in anticipation as she watched him lower his dark head. The feel of his lips closing around the hard peak sent starbursts of sensation through her. Caught up in a maelstrom of pleasure, she squirmed in his lap and felt the solid ridge of his arousal beneath her bottom.

Without conscious thought she opened her legs a little, enabling him to slide his finger into her feminine heat. The feel of him inside her drove her instantly to the brink, and she arched her hips so that he could slide deeper, gasping when he rubbed his thumb-pad lightly back and forth across her clitoris.

This was what he had wanted to do ever since Louise had walked back into his life four days ago, Dimitri acknowledged. When she had faced him in his office in Athens—a gorgeous siren in her short scarlet skirt—he had fantasised about spreading her across his desk and making hot, urgent love to her. For the past seven years she had hovered on the periphery of his mind like a lingering melody. But the flesh-and-blood woman was a thousand times more beautiful than the image of her that had occasionally flitted into his thoughts.

Ideally he would like to carry her into the bedroom and undress her slowly, take his time to explore every inch of her delectable body before he indulged in a leisurely sex session. But there wasn't a chance in hell of that happening when he was more aroused than he could remember being for a long, long time, he thought derisively. Louise's little cries of delight as he pleasured her with his fingers were fast sending him out of control.

She was breathing heavily, twisting her hips restlessly so that her bottom ground against the hardened shaft that was throbbing unbearably beneath his trousers. He felt an unexpected tug of tenderness as he studied her flushed face and the tendrils of damp hair that clung to her cheek. He controlled his own hunger and concentrated on bringing her to orgasm, moving his fingers faster in and out of her slick wetness and at the same time capturing her pebble-hard nipple in his mouth, caressing it with his tongue.

She gave a keening cry and bucked convulsively as her internal muscles tightened and relaxed again and again, each spasm making her shudder. Her head was thrown back, her golden hair spilling over the cushions, and Dimitri could not resist claiming her parted lips in a fierce kiss. He remembered how wildly responsive she had been on Eirenne. Sex with her had been amazing. He had never known another woman to be as passionate or such a generous lover.

'*Ise panemorfi,*' he murmured huskily. She was so beautiful. He was impatient to settle himself between her thighs and thrust his erection into her velvet softness.

He gripped the hem of her dress to push it up to her waist. But something was wrong. She was staring at him with an expression of horror in her eyes, and she caught hold of his wrist to prevent him from lifting her skirt.

'What is it, *glikia mou*?' he demanded raggedly, breathing hard as he struggled for control.

'Oh, God! What am I *doing*?' Louise choked, not realising that she had actually spoken the words out loud.

The sound of Dimitri's voice had shattered the sensual web he had wrapped around her and reality had reared its ugly head. She glanced down at herself, sprawled on Dimitri's knees with her legs open and the top of her dress pulled down, exposing her naked breast. Her jutting, reddened nipple seemed to taunt her, and self-disgust rolled over her with the force of a tidal wave.

Ise panemorfi...Dimitri had often murmured those words to her on Eirenne, and the memory of their brief affair and his lies made her feel sick with shame. 'Come to me,' he had said tonight—and she had immediately thrown herself at him, forgetting how he had hurt and humiliated her seven years ago.

His eyes narrowed, but his voice was carefully controlled. 'What *we're* doing hardly requires an explanation, surely?' he drawled. 'I want to make love to you, and I assume from your response to me that you want it too.'

Scorching colour tinged Louise's white face at his reminder of what a fool she had been. With trembling fingers she jerked the strap of her dress back into place and scrambled off his lap, swaying a little when she discovered that her legs felt like jelly.

'You invited me here to discuss Eirenne,' she reminded him shakily. She was horrified that for a few reckless minutes she had forgotten the reason why she had accepted his invitation to come up to his hotel suite. Without specialist treatment in America her mother would die. And if Dimitri did not buy back his family's island Louise feared she had little chance of raising the money to pay for Tina's medical costs before time ran out.

'Have you reached a decision?' she demanded.

'Not yet,' Dimitri replied curtly, struggling to hide his irritation that Louise had called a halt to their passion to talk about business. He ached low in his gut, and it was hard to think about anything other than his burning need for sexual release.

Doubts crept into his mind. Was she one of those women who liked to play games? He had met a few in his time—calculating women who used their sexual favours as a bartering tool in exchange for expensive jewellery or designer dresses.

He stared at her with mounting anger. 'You never did tell me why you're so anxious to sell the island—or why you are prepared to let it go at a knock-down price.' His eyes fell on the diamond pendant sparkling between her breasts and he could not prevent the ugly suspicions growing in his mind. 'Why do you need a large amount of money in a hurry? Are you in debt?' He ignored her sharp denial and continued relentlessly, 'I find it hard to believe that your job as a museum guide pays enough for you to be able buy valuable jewellery and designer clothes.'

'My dress was a present,' Louise told him coldly. 'I didn't pay for it. And I'm certainly not in debt.'

She was furious at his accusation, but the hard glint in his eyes warned her that he did not intend to drop the matter of why she needed to sell Eirenne. She was on dangerous ground, because she could not allow him to find out that she needed the money for her mother.

She stared at him, searching her mind frantically for a believable reason why she had offered to sell him the island. 'I admit there are a few things I need to pay for,' she muttered. 'I want to clear my student loan. And my car is ten years old and the garage has advised me that it won't cope with another winter.' Both of those statements were true, but she could not reveal to Dimitri that they were not her main priority right now.

Can't you persuade the lover who bought you your dress to buy you a new car? Dimitri thought grimly. Louise had confirmed his suspicions about her. Clearly she was the type of woman who was prepared to sell herself for personal gain—just has her mother had done. It was stupid to feel surprised or disappointed, he told himself. In many ways it made things easier, because even knowing what she was he still wanted her. And she wanted him to buy Eirenne. It felt good to know that he had the upper hand, that he was in control of the situation.

He got up from the sofa and smiled to himself when he saw a tremor run though her as he stood in front of her. 'So there *are* financial reasons why you're desperate to sell the island,' he murmured. 'Why didn't you say so from the start?'

'I'm not desperate,' Louise lied shakily, catching her bottom lip with her teeth as an image of Tina's painfully thin face flashed into her mind. She *was* desperate to help her mother, she acknowledged silently. She would do everything possible to raise the money for Tina's treatment.

'No?' Dimitri idly wound a honey-blond curl around his finger. 'So are you saying you *didn't* come up to my suite in the hope of persuading me to buy Eirenne?'

Louise stiffened. Dear God, what did he mean by *persuading*? Did he think she would…? The gleam in his olive-green eyes caused her heart to miss a beat.

'Because I *am* open to persuasion, *glikia mou*,' he drawled.

His voice lowered, and it was so deep and soft that it seemed to whisper across Louise's skin like a velvet cloak, enfolding her and drawing her to him. She could not look away from him, and her breath hitched in her throat when he lifted a hand and smoothed her hair back behind her ear. The feather-light brush of his fingertips on her neck sent a quiver through her, and she could feel the hard tips of her nipples straining beneath her silk dress, practically begging him to touch them.

From somewhere deep inside her a tiny voice of common sense pointed out that it would be madness to sink into the sensual web he was wrapping around her. Becoming involved with Dimitri would bring so many complications. But the sultry gleam in his eyes was mesmeric, inviting— inciting all sorts of exciting fantasies in her mind. Maybe she *could* persuade him to buy the island, whispered a voice in her head. Would it really be so wrong to do *anything* to save her mother's life?

She could not tear her eyes from his. He was standing so close that she could feel his breath on her cheek, and she ached for him to close the gap between them and slant his mouth over hers.

She swallowed. 'I should go.' Her voice emerged as a tremulous whisper.

'Why not stay?'

There must be a good reason. Probably dozens. But his sexy smile decimated her ability to think logically.

'I want to make love to you.' Dimitri's voice thickened with desire. He did not understand what it was about this woman that made his body ache, made him shake like a testosterone-fuelled youth anticipating his first sexual experience. All he knew was that Louise was like a fever in

his blood, and the only cure was to possess her and find
the sweet satiation his body craved.

He pulled her into his arms and his heart slammed
against his ribs when he felt the tips of her nipples pressed
against his chest. 'I want to take you to bed and undress
you, slowly. I want to lay you down and kiss every inch
of you—your mouth, your breasts, between your legs,' he
whispered in her ear. 'And then I want to take you and make
you mine, and give you more pleasure than you've ever had
with any other man.'

His voice was like honey sliding over her, and his words
made Louise melt. She was conscious of liquid warmth
between her thighs, and the throbbing ache that had only
been partially appeased when he had pleasured her with his
hands now clamoured for his complete possession.

He cupped her chin and stared into her eyes. 'I've been
honest with you. I'm not ashamed to admit how much I desire you. Now I'm asking you to be honest too.' There was
no hint of softening on his arrogant features, and he spoke
firmly, decisively. 'If you don't want to be with me tell me
now and I'll take you home.'

No other man had ever made her weak with sexual longing, Louise thought. Yet the desire blazing in Dimitri's eyes
also made her feel powerful. He had awoken feelings inside her that she hadn't felt since she was nineteen. It was
as if her sensuality had been on hold for the intervening
years, but with one kiss he had aroused a level of need in
her that only he could assuage. It was her choice whether
to stay with him or leave.

'Dimitri…'

He tightened his arms around her. 'You know you want
me, and I am burning up for you.'

The raw urgency in his voice allayed her last lingering
doubts. She wound her arms around his neck and tugged

his head down. Words were beyond her. Seven years ago he had been her first lover, and there had never been anyone else. Undoubtedly she had lost her sanity, but she could not deny her body one more night of pleasure with him. However, a sense of self-preservation held her back from telling him that her need was as great as his, and instead she reached up on tiptoe and kissed him.

Dimitri muttered something against her lips, and then he was kissing her hungrily, fiercely, desperately.

Louise cupped his face in her hands. The stubble on his jaw felt abrasive against her palms. He pushed his tongue into her mouth and slid one hand to her nape to hold her tightly to him. His other hand cupped her bottom and jerked her hard against his thighs, so that she could feel the solid ridge of his arousal jabbing her stomach.

The evidence of his desire escalated her excitement to fever-pitch. There were too many barriers between them: her dress, his shirt. She tugged at the buttons and moaned softly as she pushed the material aside and skimmed her hands over his bare chest—an olive-gold satin covered with whirls of black hair.

'Patience, *pedhaki*,' he murmured. 'We're going to do this properly, on a bed.'

He fought the temptation to strip her and position her over one arm of the sofa and lifted her into his arms to carry her into the bedroom. He set her down at the foot of the bed and turned her round so that he could undo the zip that ran the length of her spine. His hands shook and he cursed as the material caught. *Theos*, he was acting like an inexperienced boy. He dragged air into his lungs and worked the zip down to reveal the semi-transparent French knickers that covered her *derrière*. The dress slithered to the floor and he hooked his fingers in the top of her panties and pulled them down to her knees. The sight of her rounded bottom, as smooth and velvety as a ripe peach, caused his arousal to strain painfully against the restriction of his trousers. The knickers slipped to her ankles and she gave a faintly embarrassed laugh as she stepped out of them and kicked them and the black silk dress away.

Dimitri had never seen anything so erotic as Louise wearing only black hold-up stockings and stilettos. He turned her to face him and cupped her breasts in his hands, heat surging through him as he watched her pupils dilate when he rubbed his thumb-pads over her nipples.

Honey-blond curls framed her flushed face, and her eyes were the intense blue of sapphires. She was so beautiful he could just stand there looking at her. The throb of his arousal reminded him that looking wasn't enough. He wanted her to touch him, wanted to feel her cool hands caress his hot flesh.

'Undress me,' he demanded raggedly.

He sensed her faint hesitation as she reached for his belt buckle, and once she had unfastened it she hesitated again before sliding the zip of his trousers down. It suddenly hit him that she was shy, and he felt a tugging sensation in his gut when she blushed. His instincts told him that it was a while since she'd had sex. But that didn't make sense. Maybe he had been wrong about her and there was no rich lover in her life? He frowned, remembering that she had admitted her dress had been a gift. Surely only a lover would buy her sexy designer wear?

But at that moment Dimitri didn't give a damn about the dress or anything else. All he could think was that he had never been so turned on in his life and that the chances of him making love to her with any degree of finesse were distinctly unlikely.

He remembered how he had told her he wanted to kiss her everywhere, and he kept his promise—starting with her mouth. With practised efficiency he slipped off his shoes, socks and trousers, and then drew her into his arms and claimed her lips. His excitement intensified when she responded instantly. She was an intriguing mix of diffidence and boldness, and when she tentatively pushed her tongue into his mouth he groaned and crushed her against him, the last vestiges of his restraint decimated by his savage need to possess her.

It was an amazing bed, Louise thought as Dimitri lifted her and laid her on the mattress. She looked up at the silvery-grey silk canopy above her head. The satin bedspread she was lying on felt decadently sensual against her skin, but the touch of Dimitri's naked body aroused her even more. She hadn't been aware of him stripping off his underwear, and as he knelt over her she could not help but stare at his massive erection.

She felt a faint flicker of trepidation when she imagined taking him inside her. She had done so once before, she reminded herself, albeit seven years ago. Giving her virginity to him had been a beautiful experience, and the quivering sensation in the pit of her stomach was a sign that her body was impatient for him to make love to her with unrestrained passion.

But first it seemed that he wanted to play—to tease and tantalise her. He slipped off her shoes and then peeled her stockings down her legs before he started to kiss her. Within minutes of him trailing his mouth over every dip and curve of her body she was breathing hard and trembling with anticipation.

'Please…' she whispered when he finally lifted his mouth from hers after a kiss that had plundered her soul. She was on fire, and molten heat flooded between her thighs in readiness for his possession.

'I intend to please you, *glikia.*'

The quiet intent in his voice escalated her excitement, and she caught her breath when he cradled her breasts in his big palms and bent his head to kiss one nipple and then the other, curling his tongue around each tight bud and lapping her, licking her, until the pleasure was almost too much to bear. She arched her hips in instinctive invitation. He accepted as he moved down her body and pushed her legs open so that he could bestow the most intimate kiss of all.

She bucked and shook, and he laughed softly and held her firmly while he dipped his tongue into her honeyed sweetness. He brought her to the edge, held her there, but when she pleaded for him never to stop he positioned himself over her, supporting his weight on his elbows.

'Touch me,' he bade her harshly, and groaned when she obeyed and circled him with her slender hands.

He loved the way she blushed—her pink cheeks and soft smile reminded him of the girl who had given herself to him so shyly and yet with gut-wrenching eagerness on Eirenne. Common sense told him that his instincts had to be wrong, and she must have had other lovers apart from him. But not many, he guessed, and perhaps not for a while. She was still a little hesitant, and seemed content for him to take the lead. That suited him fine, Dimitri thought, because he was too fired up to wait any longer.

There were condoms in the bedside drawer—thankfully he always carried them with him. Not that he had expected he would need them when he had come to Paris. He hadn't planned to take Louise to bed, but deep down he *had* hoped, he admitted to himself. There was something between them that defied explanation—a sense that she belonged to him, which was curious because he'd never felt possessive about other women he'd slept with.

The moment had come. Louise knew from the darkness of Dimitri's eyes that the time for foreplay was over. But she felt no fear or doubt, only a fierce joy as she stared at his face and saw the younger man she had known on Eirenne as well as the man he was now. They were one and the same—the Dimitri she had been falling in love with many years ago and the Dimitri who, if she was not on her guard, could easily threaten her heart now.

He kissed her lips softly, sweetly, so that tears filled her eyes. His hands were gentle as he spread her legs wider and slowly lowered himself onto her. She felt the tip of his penis push against her, and as he eased into her with exquisite care his eyes locked with hers and she felt that their souls as well as their bodies were joined.

'Are you all right? Is it hurting?' She was so hot and tight it was all he could do not to explode instantly, Dimitri acknowledged, gritting his teeth as he fought for control.

'No, it's fine…it's good.' *It's unbelievably wonderful,* Louise added silently. 'Really,' she assured him, and kissed away the slight frown between his brows. She lifted her hips. 'I want you to…'

Her words died away as he slid deeper, filling her, completing her. He seemed to know exactly what she wanted, and he withdrew and slid deep again, each thrust more intense than the last, driving her relentlessly on a heart-stopping journey towards a place that she sensed was there but remained frustratingly out of her reach.

'Dimitri…' She gripped his shoulders and felt the sheen of sweat on his skin. She arched up to meet the rhythmic strokes of his body and gasped as he held her hips and drove into her harder, faster, until the world spun out of control.

He claimed her mouth and her heart leapt when she sensed tenderness as well as passion in his kiss.

'Relax and let it happen,' he murmured.

And then it did happen, and the beauty of it took her breath away. He thrust powerfully, the deepest yet, and the hot, throbbing ache in her pelvis suddenly imploded, sending wave after tumultuous wave of pleasure through her. She sank into the exquisite ecstasy of her orgasm, drowned in its tidal force, and sobbed his name as the waves continued to pound her.

Her internal muscles convulsed around him, squeezed and released him in frantic spasms that blew Dimitri's mind. He paused, every sinew straining as he sought to prolong the journey and delay the pleasure he knew was ahead for just a few seconds longer. The anticipation of it clawed in his gut. He took a shuddering breath, and as he stared down at Louise's rose-flushed face he thought how lovely she was. No other woman had ever made him feel this way—as if he was a king and could conquer the world. He couldn't hold on, and he made a harsh, primitive sound in his throat at the moment of release before he sank into the haven of her arms and she cradled his head on her breasts.

CHAPTER SIX

LOUISE opened her eyes and stared at the grey silk drapes around the bed. She was instantly awake as memories of the previous night flooded her mind. She had never slept in a four-poster before, or in a bed of this size. Two people could sleep in a bed this big and never touch each other. But that hadn't happened with her and Dimitri.

They had touched and kissed and caressed each other and made love twice during the night—three times, actually. But the last time had been just before dawn, when the sky outside had lightened from indigo to purple but the stars had yet to go out.

Now the cool grey light of early morning was filtering through the half-open curtains, and the new day brought with it big doubts about whether it had been wise to spend the night with a man who was to all intents and purposes a stranger. She had thought she had known him seven years ago, but their brief relationship had been based on lies. The reality was that she did not know Dimitri Kalakos at all.

The feverish excitement that had overwhelmed her last night had faded and common sense had returned. Sleeping with him had not been wise at all, said a voice in her head. It had complicated everything.

She turned her head to study him. He was lying on his front, his head pillowed on his arms and his face turned towards her. His thick, dark eyelashes were fanned against his cheeks and Louise's gaze lingered on the sensual curve of his mouth. She felt a little tug of emotion as she watched him sleeping. He looked relaxed. The fine lines around his eyes had smoothed out and he looked more like the younger Dimitri she had met on Eirenne.

He must have been a beautiful child. Her heart ached as she wondered whether their child would have resembled him. If she had had a son, he would be six years old now. She pictured a wiry, olive-skinned little boy, with a mass of dark hair and olive-green eyes, a cheeky grin and a streak of daring that would inevitably get him into trouble from time to time.

Sadness hit her like a blow to her chest. It did not matter how many times she told herself it was stupid to grieve for a child who had never been born. The loss of her baby still hurt after all this time, and being with Dimitri again made the memories so much more intense.

She wondered what he would have been like as a father. *If he had stuck around*, pointed out the voice in her head. There was no guarantee he would have supported her. If her pregnancy had continued she would have contacted him and told him she was expecting his baby, but perhaps he would have rejected his child as her father had rejected her.

The box of condoms on the bedside table was a mocking reminder of their night of physical pleasure. She could only be thankful he had remembered to use protection. She felt ashamed that in the heat of the moment contraception hadn't crossed her mind. How awful was that? she berated herself. Hadn't one unplanned pregnancy been enough? It was true that even if she *had* had unprotected sex her chances of conceiving were slim after the problems she'd suffered with her first pregnancy. But there was no escaping the fact that last night she had behaved utterly irresponsibly.

She stared up at the canopy above the bed and chewed on her bottom lip. Dimitri had told her he was returning to Greece later today. He was a notorious playboy and in all likelihood regarded last night as a one-night stand. What was the protocol when you woke up in bed with a man you'd had casual sex with? she wondered. Would he offer her breakfast and ring Room Service? Or would he be impatient for her to leave and arrange a taxi to take her home?

She couldn't do it, she thought bleakly. She could not go through with the charade of acting as though spending the night in a guy's hotel bedroom was something she did regularly. It was not that she was ashamed of sleeping with him; she was a free and single female living in the twenty-first century and she would not judge any woman for enjoying sex without strings. It was just that it wasn't *her*. She had certain rules she lived by, and last night she had broken all of them.

Another thought struck her. Had she managed to *persuade* him to buy Eirenne? She paled. What had she been thinking last night? The truth was she had not been thinking at all, but had been swept away by passion tinged with evocative memories of their relationship years ago. Now, in the cold light of day, she could not bear for him to believe that she had followed in her mother's footsteps and become the type of woman who was prepared to sell herself for financial gain—even if it was not for her own gain.

It suddenly became imperative that she left before Dimitri woke up. She couldn't face him when her emotions were all over the place. Taking care not to disturb him, she slid out of bed and winced when she discovered muscles she had not known existed. The ache inside her was worse. She felt empty and a little bit sick as she gathered up her clothes from the floor and crept into the bathroom.

* * *

The clock on the bedside table flashed 9:13 a.m. As Dimitri stared at the red digits they changed to 9:14. *Theos!* He sat up and raked a hand through his hair. He had never stayed in bed until a quarter past nine in his life—or not to sleep, anyway. On rare occasions he invited a mistress to stay the night with him—the single benefit being that he could have sex the following morning. Last night had been one of those occasions, but it had backfired, because from the empty space in the bed beside him and the strangely muted silence of the hotel suite it appeared that Louise had already left.

Frowning, he flicked back the sheets and padded into the bathroom. The absence of the dress, shoes and underwear that last night had been strewn across the floor confirmed her disappearance. Maybe she'd gone to work, he mused as he stepped into the shower. He felt irritated that she had not woken him before she left. He was uncomfortable with the idea that she might have watched him sleeping, and that was crazy because he had never felt vulnerable in his life.

His bad mood was due to frustration that he hadn't stirred first and kissed her awake, he decided. He'd bet she looked gorgeous first thing: sleepily sexy, with her hair all mussed and her mouth all soft and moist and eager. He would have liked to trail his lips down to her breasts and tease her dusky pink nipples until she made that little whimpering moan she had made last night. Hell, he would have liked to roll her beneath him and ease his swollen shaft into her, taking them both on an early-morning ride and watching her come apart in his arms.

He felt himself harden and turned the shower's temperature setting to cold to cool his desire. There would be other mornings—and definitely other nights. He was not a fan of long-distance affairs, but the flight time between Athens and Paris was only three hours and it would be easy enough to meet up with Louise at weekends.

In many ways the fact that they did not live in the same city was good, he thought as he reached for a towel. There was less danger that their affair would slip into complacency and become boring. He could smell the lingering scent of her perfume when he walked back into the bedroom, and he kept picturing her lying naked on the satin sheets as he lowered himself onto her. The thought struck him as he donned chinos and a black polo shirt that he was disappointed that she had gone without saying goodbye or arranging when they would next meet.

Dimitri frowned again. The way she had sneaked out like that—it was as if she did not care if she ever saw him again. Maybe she didn't. He was conscious of a peculiar sinking feeling in his stomach, and felt irritated with himself. Hell, how many times had he spent the night with a woman and in the morning made vague assurances about calling her that he had no intention of keeping? The fact that Louise hadn't acted like a clinging vine should be cause for celebration, not regret.

He slipped on his jacket and checked his cell phone. There were no messages, but he had her number. He would give her a call later. Sure, he wanted to see her again, but he didn't want to appear too keen.

The humiliation of scurrying out of a five-star hotel at dawn, wearing a dress that she had clearly worn the previous evening, was something Louise doubted she would forget in a hurry. The doorman's face had been inscrutable, but she had been painfully aware that her wild hair, old make-up and bare legs—she hadn't wasted time pulling on her stockings—had all indicated that she had spent the night in bed with a lover, and the dark circles beneath her eyes were proof that she'd had very little sleep.

Madeleine stared at her reproachfully when she let herself into the apartment, and showed her disapproval by remaining regally on her cushion on the windowsill.

'I know, I know.' Louise groaned. 'I must have taken leave of my senses. But it won't happen again.'

Dimitri would be back in Athens in a few hours. If—as she hoped and prayed—he agreed to buy Eirenne, the sale would be dealt with by their respective lawyers and there was no reason why they should ever meet again.

She headed straight for the shower and stood beneath the spray for ages, as if she could wash the touch of his hands from her skin. Images kept pushing into her mind of the way he had made love to her—with the consummate skill of a renowned playboy but also with an unexpected gentleness. It made her heart ache when she recalled the soft endearments he had whispered in Greek as she had lain spent and utterly sated in his arms...

A message on her answer-machine drove Dimitri and every other thought from her head. The consultant in charge of her mother's care was voicing his concerns that Tina's condition had worsened, and he suggested that Louise should meet with him as soon as possible.

The hospital was in a suburb of Paris. She found her mother dozing when she slipped into her private room, and as she sat by the bed she noted with a pang of dread that Tina had lost more weight and her skin was ashen. The scarf tied around her head hid the fact that she had lost her hair after chemotherapy. Tears stung Louise's eyes as she remembered Tina's blond beehive hairstyle. How cruel was this disease that had robbed her mother of her looks and seemed intent on stealing her life.

'Loulou?' Tina's eyes fluttered open.

'I'm here.' She wished she could call her mother 'Mum', but Tina had always insisted that Louise should use her Christian name.

'It makes me seem old to have a teenager address me as Mum,' Tina had complained.

For years she had lied about her age and told her lovers that she was twenty-eight.

Louise sighed and curled her fingers around Tina's bony hand. 'I'm sorry I didn't visit yesterday. I worked until late, and then I...' She faltered when she thought of what she had done after work. 'I went out to dinner.'

A gleam of curiosity flickered in her mother's eyes. 'With a boyfriend?' She studied Louise. 'I'm glad you've started to make more effort with your appearance. The suit you're wearing is gorgeous. You've got a great figure and it's about time you started to show it off. That's the only way to attract a man.'

Louise gave a wry smile, but did not explain that she was wearing one of Benoit's designs because she knew her mother liked her to dress well. 'I'm not trying to attract a man,' she murmured. 'I'm too involved with my job. Did I tell you I've applied for a position as an assistant curator in the Department of Paintings at the Louvre?'

Tina had closed her eyes, but after a moment she opened them again. 'I'm pleased you've got a good career. I always hoped you would. Not like me—I never trained in anything.'

Talking seemed to tire her and she fell silent for a few minutes. Louise was just about to tiptoe from the room when Tina spoke again.

'Kostas was in love with me, and I cared about him. He was the only one. All the others just wanted me for one thing. It boosted their egos to have a mistress, but they never thought about me as a person and after a while I stopped hoping they would. I used them like they used me.'

Louise swallowed the lump in her throat. She had never realised before that her mother had been looking for love with all those different men. In the end she had found it with Kostas Kalakos, but their relationship had hurt so many other people—especially Kostas's wife and family. She understood why Dimitri despised Tina, she thought bleakly.

'The tumour is growing quicker than we had expected,' explained Alain Duval, the cancer specialist who was caring for Tina, after he'd invited Louise into his office. 'I can't guarantee that the pioneering treatment offered at our associate hospital in Massachusetts would be successful, but it *is* your mother's only chance. Soon the opportunity for that chance will be lost,' he added quietly.

'How long does she have before time runs out for her to have the treatment?' Louise asked tensely.

'A few weeks at most. Ideally she needs to start the newly developed form of radiation therapy immediately. I appreciate that medical costs in the United States are high, and that your mother does not have health insurance that would cover the costs. But if there is any way at all that you could raise the money I suggest you do so without delay.'

If *only* Dimitri would agree to buy Eirenne. She could not give him any more time to make up his mind, Louise thought frantically. She prayed he had not left Paris. As soon as she had finished at the hospital she would go back to his hotel and plead with him to give her an answer.

Her mind whirled. If he refused to buy the island she would instruct the estate agent to advertise for a buyer. In the meantime she would try to arrange a temporary loan. But she had already asked the bank once and her request had been refused. Panic churned in her stomach.

'I'm in the process of selling some assets to cover the medical expenses,' she explained to the consultant. 'The money should be available soon. But I want my mother to begin the treatment right away.'

'I can make arrangements for her to be transferred

to the U.S. But I have to advise you that the hospital in Massachusetts is unlikely to start Madame Hobbs's treatment until they have assurance that all her medical costs can be covered,' Alain Duval explained gently. 'You will also need to pay for your mother's flight on an air ambulance.' He checked his computer screen and scribbled down a figure. 'This is the amount you'll need to find initially.'

There was only one other way she could raise any kind of capital.

Louise nodded resolutely. 'I'll organise it now.'

Her grandmother Céline would have approved, she told herself a few hours later when she walked out of the jeweller's shop. The jeweller had honoured the price that he had originally valued the diamond *fleur-de-lis*, and had also bought the last few pieces of Tina's jewellery. Louise hoped her mother would forgive her. Tina adored her jewels, but life was more valuable than a few baubles.

Having delivered a cheque to Alain Duval, and learned that Tina would be flown to Massachusetts once the hospital had received assurance that her medical costs would be met, Louise felt as if her emotions had been put through a mangle. She had phoned Dimitri's hotel and learned that he had not yet checked out, but was unavailable to speak to her.

The prospect of meeting him again made her heart sink. But she *had* to get an answer from him. First, though, she decided to go back to her flat to feed Madeleine and try and drum up some courage before she paid him a visit.

The lift in the apartment block only went as far as the fifth floor. Louise trudged up the narrow flight of stairs leading to the eaves of the building, feeling utterly drained. Reaction to the events of the past twenty-four hours had set in. She was still trying to come to terms with the fact that she had slept with Dimitri, and she was desperately worried about her mother.

The sound of footsteps from above warned her that one of her neighbours was coming down the stairs, and she shrank against the wall to allow them to pass.

'Where in hell's name have you been all day?'

Dimitri came round the bend in the staircase and strode towards her, his face furious and beautiful, with his olive-gold skin stretched taut across his slashing cheekbones, his green eyes spitting fire.

The shock of his appearance was the last straw. Louise stared at him wordlessly.

'Why did you shoot off like that this morning?' The question had been bugging Dimitri all day. 'I tried ringing you a dozen times but you didn't answer.'

'I switched off my phone at the...' Just in time she stopped herself from saying *hospital*, and coloured guiltily. 'I went to see a...friend, and turned my phone off.'

'I assumed you had left early to go to the museum, but when I couldn't get hold of you I checked at the Louvre and was told that you weren't scheduled to work today.' Dimitri's eyes narrowed when Louise refused to meet his gaze. 'You ran, didn't you? What was it?' he queried sardonically. 'Self-recrimination after the night before?'

She flushed. 'You told me you were returning to Athens today. It just seemed easier to avoid any awkwardness. I mean...' She bit her lip. 'We both know last night didn't mean anything.'

'Do we?' His face was unreadable.

What friend had she rushed off to visit? Dimitri wondered. She seemed cagey. Had she gone to see a lover—perhaps to give an excuse for where she had spent the previous night? And how was it that she was wearing another Benoit Besson outfit?

He was annoyed that he had felt concerned when he'd been unable to contact her. She was not a child, and certainly not his responsibility, he reminded himself. His irritation increased when he felt his body's predictable reaction as he raked his eyes over her champagne-coloured pencil skirt and the matching jacket with its nipped-in waist that emphasised the firm swell of her breasts. Her hair was swept into a chignon and her face discreetly made-up. The combination of cool elegance and simmering sensuality that she projected heated his blood to boiling point. No woman had ever run out on him before, and if he was honest his ego had been dented by Louise's abrupt departure from his bed that morning, he acknowledged grimly.

Louise could not define Dimitri's expression and she was too weary to try. 'What are you doing here, anyway?' she muttered.

He looked dangerously seductive in casual clothes that bore the hallmarks of superb tailoring. His black polo shirt clung to the hard ridges of his abdominal muscles and his dark hair brushed the collar of his tan leather jacket. For a crazy moment she almost gave in to the temptation to fling herself against his broad chest and absorb some of his strength.

A thought hit her and she drew a sharp breath. 'Have you made a decision about the island?'

'I have, but a public stairway is not the place to discuss it. I believe your apartment is on the top floor?'

Her legs were shaking, Louise discovered as she led the way up the stairs and along the hallway to her flat. A sense of dread settled like a lead weight in her stomach. Dimitri did not know it, but he held her mother's life in his hands.

'Please—come in.' She opened the front door and ushered him into her home, hating her body's involuntary reaction when he brushed against her. Why *him*? she thought bitterly. Why was he the only man she had ever met who could turn her brain to mush and make her feel like a hormonal adolescent instead of the intelligent woman she knew was?

Entering Louise's flat was like stepping into a doll's house, Dimitri thought as he was forced to duck to avoid bumping his head on the doorframe. An estate agent would probably describe the apartment as a bijou residence, but that was a euphemism for small. It occurred to him that if Louise did live with some rich lover he must be a midget.

He followed her into the living room and saw no signs of a male influence in the pretty but decidedly feminine décor. A door led into what he could see was an equally tiny bedroom. The apartment was functional but hardly luxurious, and he felt certain that Louise lived alone.

Not completely alone, he amended as his eyes settled on the exotic-looking cat which was regarding him suspiciously from the windowsill.

'That's Madeleine,' Louise told him, following his gaze. 'I got her from the cat rescue centre and she's wary of strangers.'

He glanced around the room. The colour scheme of white and powder-blue was charming, but nothing could disguise the fact that the apartment was no bigger than a shoebox.

'It's not what I was expecting,' he said, frowning. When Louise had told him she lived in the centre of Paris he had envisaged a grand, opulent apartment. 'I thought you would live somewhere bigger and more expensive, frankly.'

'I can't afford the rent on a bigger place. This is fine for me and Madeleine.'

'Surely your mother could contribute towards the costs of renting or even buying a larger apartment? After all, she inherited a sizeable fortune from my father.'

'I have never touched a penny of Kostas's money,' Louise said sharply.

She had caught the note of bitterness in Dimitri's voice

and in all fairness could not blame him for it. Her mother's affair with his father hovered like a spectre between them. She dared not reveal that the reason she was so anxious for him to buy Eirenne was because Tina had frittered away the inheritance Kostas had left her.

She twisted her hands together, unaware that Dimitri had noticed the betraying gesture. 'You said you had made a decision,' she reminded him.

Why was she so tense? he wondered. It was obvious she was desperate for him to agree to a deal on Eirenne, but he still did not know *why* she needed the money so urgently. The explanation she'd given about wanting to pay off her student loan wasn't believable, and once again he came back to the idea that she was in debt. Her mother had been facing bankruptcy just before she had met his father, he remembered. Tina had not been a good role model when it came to financial matters—or personal integrity, he thought grimly. Was it any surprise that Louise seemed to be following in her mother's footsteps?

But what did it matter? Dimitri asked himself. He wanted Eirenne and he wanted Louise, and he was determined to have both. One night with her had not satisfied his desire and he had decided that the only way to get her out of his system was to make her his mistress until his fascination with her faded. He had a short attention span where women were concerned, and he was sure it would not take long before he was bored of her.

He glanced at her and felt a white-hot surge of lust as he imagined stripping off the elegant suit and the lace-edged camisole visible beneath her jacket. Was she wearing a bra? No matter—he would quickly remove it so that he could cup her voluptuous breasts in his hands. Then he would kiss her nipples, lick them and tease them with his tongue, until they hardened and she whimpered and begged him to make love to her as she had done last night…

His nostrils flared as he inhaled sharply. He turned towards the window and pretended to study the view of Paris rooftops while he endeavoured to bring his body under control.

'I am prepared to pay your asking price of one million pounds for Eirenne.'

'Thank God!'

She spoke the words beneath her breath but Dimitri heard her, heard the raw emotion in her voice, and he flicked his head round to see her sink down onto the sofa as if her legs would not support her.

'That's…great news.' Louise frantically fought for composure as relief flooded through her. The one thought pounding in her head was that now she could phone Alain Duval and tell him to arrange for her mother to be flown to America to begin the treatment immediately.

'There is a condition.'

Dimitri's clipped statement seemed to reverberate off the walls. Louise shot him a lightning glance, and something about his calculating expression unnerved her. She licked her dry lips.

'What…condition?'

'You will return to Athens with me.'

Why was her heart thudding so erratically beneath her ribs? she wondered. After all, Dimitri had not made an unreasonable request.

She stood up and faced him across her tiny sitting room. 'I suppose it will be necessary for me to sign a sales contract. Of course I will fly to Athens when the paperwork has been prepared,' she assured him. 'But I imagine it will take at least a few days before your lawyers are ready to finalise the deal.'

He shrugged. 'Probably. But that's not what I meant.' He walked towards her, his intent gaze holding her prisoner. 'I want *you*, Louise—to share my bed every night until I have sated my desire for you. Let's say for a couple of weeks.' His smile was deeply cynical. 'I have a low boredom threshold, and experience tells me that my interest will wane fairly quickly when you are available around the clock.'

'Available?' she choked furiously. His suggestion was so shockingly outrageous that she almost thought he was joking—but the hard gleam in his eyes warned her he was deadly serious. 'Do you really expect me to play the role of your…your *concubine*? Always on hand to serve you and satisfy your sexual demands?'

She paused to drag oxygen into her lungs, and opened her mouth to tell him in succinct terms just what she thought of his suggestion. He cut her off before she could speak.

'If you want me to buy Eirenne then, yes, that's exactly what I expect.'

Stunned by the finality of his words, she felt her defiance crumble. 'That's blackmail,' she whispered.

He gave her an impatient look. 'Oh, come on, *glikia*. It's a little too late to play the innocent. You were a wildcat last night and you know damn well you're as hungry as I am.'

Before she had time to guess his intention Dimitri shot out a hand and unfastened the single button on her jacket, before flicking the material aside to reveal the sheer camisole she was wearing beneath it.

'Even if you want to deny it, your body betrays you—see?' he taunted, a sardonic smile lifting the corners of his mouth as he deliberately trailed a finger down one breast and over the pebble-hard nipple jutting provocatively against its silk covering. 'Why do you wear a bra when your breasts are so firm? While you are my mistress I demand that you will go braless.'

'You can go to hell!' The soft mockery in Dimitri's voice released Louise from the sexual spell he had cast on her. She despised him, but she despised herself more for her shameful inability to resist him. 'I refuse to be any man's mistress, and I'd rather sell my soul to the devil than agree to your despicable suggestion.'

'Then the deal is off,' he said calmly, regarding her flushed face and anger-bright eyes with a detached air that caused Louise to clench her fists. 'I wish you well in finding another buyer for Eirenne.'

'You don't mean that. You're calling my bluff,' she blurted, panic rising inside her when he strolled towards the door. 'Dimitri...*please*! There has to be a way we can reach an agreement.'

She had no right to look hurt, Dimitri told himself, determined to ignore the tug on his insides when he glimpsed tears in her eyes. She had proved last night that she was a woman like her mother—willing to sell herself for the right price. He would not be taken in by the air of vulnerability that reminded him of the girl he had known years ago.

'I've explained my terms—it's up to you whether you agree them.' He glanced at his watch. 'My private jet is on standby at Orly airport and my chauffeur is waiting in the car. If you're coming with me, you have precisely ten minutes to pack.'

'For God's sake—I have a job. I can't just give it up.' Louise glared at him, her temper simmering at his sheer arrogance.

'You must be allowed to take annual leave?'

'It will be difficult at such short notice.' But not impossible, Louise acknowledged silently. A few weeks ago she had explained the situation with her mother to her manager and arranged to take time off if the need arose. There would not be a problem at work.

The problem was with herself, she admitted. She resented with every fibre of her being the idea of becoming Dimitri's mistress—but what choice did she have? she thought bleakly. To refuse him would be to sign her mother's death warrant. The only way to raise the money for Tina's cancer treatment quickly was to sell Dimitri the island. And maybe he had a point. Maybe being forced to spend time with him, to live with him and share his bed every night, would free her from his sensual spell.

She drew a shaky breath, hardly able to believe what she was about to do. The sight of him reaching for the door handle prompted her to speak.

'All right—I agree to your terms. But I want your signed confirmation that you will pay one million pounds for Eirenne, and that you will transfer the money to me as soon as possible.' She crossed to the bureau and took out a sheet of paper and a pen which she held out to him. 'Do it now—before we leave.'

He studied her speculatively for a moment, but made no comment as he strolled back into the room and took the blank paper from her. Resting it on the lid of the bureau, he scribbled a few lines, added his signature, and handed it back to her.

Louise scanned what he had written and nodded. She did not know how legally binding the agreement was, but she felt better for having something more than his spoken promise. Promises, as she knew too well, could be broken.

She lifted her head, and her heart thudded when she glimpsed the unguarded desire in his glinting gaze. It took every ounce of her will-power to say in a dignified tone, 'I'll go and pack.'

'In a minute.' His arm snaked around her waist and he jerked her towards him. 'First I'd also like confirmation of our agreement,' he drawled as he lowered his head.

His kiss was hard, hungry, demanding her response. He caught hold of her chin and pushed his tongue into her mouth to explore her with devastating eroticism until she was trembling and pliant in his arms. Louise hated herself for capitulating to him, but she could not deny him when molten heat was surging through her veins and she was aware of nothing but the feel of his hand on her bare breast as he slid it beneath her camisole and bra and rolled her nipple between his fingers.

Her mouth was swollen when he finally released her, and she dragged her clothes back into place with shaking hands while he watched with cool detachment.

'I think we understand one another,' he murmured. 'Hurry up and get your things together, I have a busy schedule and I should have left Paris hours ago. One other thing.' He halted her as she began to walk into her bedroom. 'The suit you are wearing—where did you buy it?'

'I didn't—it was given to me.' She gave him a puzzled look. 'Why do you ask?'

'I was merely curious.'

His tone was bland, yet Louise sensed that he was angry although she had no idea why. A movement from the windowsill caught her attention.

'Madeleine!' She was horrified that she had momentarily forgotten about the cat. 'What am I going to do about her?'

'Can you arrange for one of your friends to look after her while you're away?'

She ran a mental check-list of her closest friends and shook her head. Nicole had recently given birth to her first baby, Pascale was on her honeymoon, and Monique had just started a new job. Louise felt reluctant to bother her. Even Benoit was not around.

'The neighbour who sometimes feeds Madeleine for me is away.'

'Then you'll have to put her in a cattery.' Dimitri did not bother to disguise his growing impatience.

'Absolutely not,' Louise told him fiercely. 'Madeleine was abandoned by her previous owner and I'm not going to allow her to feel abandoned for a second time. She'll have to come with us. Her carrier is in the kitchen.'

Dimitri was tempted to remind her that she was not in a position to dictate terms, but the determined gleam in Louise's eyes told him she would fight to the death for the sake of her pet and he did not have time for any further delays. He caught hold of her arm as she walked past him.

'I'll see to the goddamned cat while you collect your things.'

'I doubt you'll manage. I told you—she doesn't like strangers.'

Louise watched him walk back to the windowsill and stretch out a hand towards Madeleine. *Bite him*, she willed. But, to her amazement, the cat arched her back and purred blissfully as Dimitri stroked her ears. Of course. She had underestimated his ability to charm all members of the female sex—human and animal, she thought bitterly. It was stupid, but Madeleine's acceptance of him felt like a betrayal, and tears stung Louise's eyes as she marched into her bedroom and dragged a suitcase from the wardrobe.

CHAPTER SEVEN

Louise had travelled by private jet on a few occasions when her mother had been Kostas Kalakos's mistress. As she glanced around the luxurious cabin of Dimitri's plane she was reminded of how much Tina had relished the glamorous lifestyle she had enjoyed with her billionaire lover. Her mother had sold herself to the highest bidder, she thought bleakly. Tina had insisted she'd loved Kostas, but there was no doubt she had also loved his money.

Was what she was doing any better? Louise asked herself. The stark truth was that she had agreed to sell her body to Dimitri for one million pounds. He did not know and must never discover that she intended to use the money to save the life of the woman he hated and blamed for destroying his family.

She glanced at him, sitting beside her on one of the plush white leather chairs, and felt the familiar lurch of her heart as she studied his sculpted features. Would she have agreed to be his mistress if she hadn't found him so attractive? The thought sat uncomfortably with her and she tried to blank it out and concentrate on the only reason why she was flying to Athens with him. Tina.

The journey had so far been effortless—Dimitri's chauffeur-driven limousine had whisked them to the airport, where they had boarded his jet, and two impossibly

elegant stewardesses had served them champagne as soon
as the plane had soared into the sky. The signature of ex-
treme wealth was everywhere—not simply in his material
possessions but in the deferential way people treated him,
Louise mused. She did not belong in Dimitri's world, but
for the next two weeks she would live with him and share
his bed every night.

Nervous tension churned in her stomach. Part of her
wanted to scream that she could not go through with it, that
she was not a woman like her mother. But it was for her
mother's sake that she had agreed to Dimitri's demands,
and she would stick to her side of the deal because it was
the only way she could give Tina a chance to beat the disease that threatened her life.

She tore her gaze from him to stare out of the window
as the plane circled above Athens airport, unaware that her
pensive expression was causing him to frown.

Despite her sophisticated clothes Louise looked young
and curiously vulnerable, Dimitri brooded. He was reminded of the innocent girl Loulou, whom he had known
years ago, and was momentarily assailed by doubts. Was
she *really* a cynical gold-digger like her mother, or could
he have misjudged her? Her agreement to be his mistress
in return for a million pounds surely answered that question, he thought grimly.

'We should land in five minutes.'

She made no comment and his irritation grew. 'You're
very quiet. In fact you've barely spoken a word since we
left Paris. What's the matter?'

Louise refused to admit that she felt as nervous as hell.
Through the window she could see the airport runway
grow bigger as the plane descended. It was hard to believe
that less than a week ago she had made this same trip to
Athens—although on an economy flight. When she had

left Dimitri's office she had felt optimistic that he would agree to buy Eirenne, but she could not have foreseen the condition he would impose.

She turned her head and met his hard gaze. If only she was immune to his sexy charm, but the acceleration of her heartbeat was a shameful reminder of how much he affected her. Bravado was her only defence against him.

'I didn't realise you expected me to entertain you outside of the bedroom.'

His smile faded and his jaw hardened. 'I don't. The knowledge that you will spend every night of the next two weeks naked and *willing* in my bed is all I want from you, *glikia*.'

She flushed at the predatory gleam in his eyes and tried not to feel hurt by his sarcasm. Years ago he had called her *glikia mou*—my darling—and meant it. At least she had believed he had. But her illusion that he cared about her had been shattered when she'd discovered he had only feigned interest in her to upset her mother.

The voice of the pilot asking them to fasten their seatbelts prior to landing was a welcome distraction, but as the plane touched down Louise could not shake off the feeling that she was trapped in a nightmare—destined to spend the coming weeks as the mistress of a man who clearly only regarded her as a sexual plaything.

Dimitri lived in an exclusive suburb to the north-east of Athens, where luxurious villas were surrounded by landscaped gardens. Louise's tension had increased with every mile during the short journey from the airport, and as the car swept onto a gravel driveway and electric gates closed smoothly behind them she instantly felt as though she was a prisoner.

His house certainly did not resemble a prison, she acknowledged. It was dusk, but even though the light was fading she could not fail to appreciate the beauty of Dimitri's home. Built in a neoclassical style, it had graceful arches and elegant pillars. The tall windows must allow light to flood into the rooms, she thought as she climbed the sweeping stone staircase leading up to the front door. The light coral-coloured walls reminded Louise of the old villa on Eirenne where she and Dimitri had first become lovers, a lifetime ago it seemed, and she felt a sharp pang as memories flooded her mind.

The interior décor of the house reflected the timeless elegance of its exterior. The spacious high-ceilinged rooms were painted in neutral tones, and the plush sofas and pale oak furnishings were discreetly expensive. It was a home rather than a show house, she mused, as he gave her a tour of the ground-floor rooms.

'*Your* home is not what I had expected either,' she told him, recalling his surprise when he had looked around the tiny sitting room of her flat in Paris.

'What were you expecting it to be like?'

'I don't know—a typical bachelor pad, I suppose. Minimalist chic meets playboy mansion, with lots of seductive lighting and leopard-print throws.'

He threw back his head and laughed—a deep, mellow sound that eased the tension between them.

'*Thee mou*, I hope you will think my home more tasteful than that. I promise you won't find animal print of any description here. I grew up here,' he explained. 'This was the family home until my parents split up. My father gave my mother the house as part of the divorce settlement, and when she died she left it to me.'

He glanced around the room they were standing in, which was at the front of the house, overlooking the drive.

'This was the playroom when my sister and I were children. Every evening I used to kneel on the windowsill and watch for my father's car when he came home from work, and then I would rush out to meet him and beg him to play football with me.' Dimitri paused and stared out of the window. 'He always did. However tired he was after a long day at the office, he always had time for me.' He grimaced. 'I wish things hadn't changed.'

Louise knew he meant that he wished his father had not met her mother and felt guilty, even though she could not have prevented Tina's affair with Kostas. In her mind she pictured a little boy watching excitedly for his father to return home. But although the boy resembled Dimitri it was *their* child she imagined. If her pregnancy had been successful they might now have a son, she thought wistfully. Perhaps they would have lived here in this house as a family—maybe even had other children.

The familiar ache of grief swept through her and she bit her lip to stop herself from blurting out the truth to him. There was no point in telling him about the baby she had lost. It was stupid to keep thinking about it and tormenting herself with daydreams of what might have been. There was a good chance that Dimitri would not have wanted their child—as he had not wanted *her*—and she would have spent the past six years as a single mother with all the problems that entailed, she reminded herself.

Dimitri swung away from the window and frowned when he saw Louise's pale face. She looked fragile, with dark shadows under her eyes, and once again he felt a prickle of doubt about his decision to bring her to Athens. He had not forced her, he reminded himself. She was here of her own free will because she wanted something from him—namely for him to buy the island that should have been his.

'You look as though you could do with something to eat,' he said abruptly. 'Dinner should be ready.'

Louise's insides churned at the prospect of food, but she followed him across the hall and into the dining room, where the table had been set for them.

'This is my butler, Joseph.' Dimitri introduced the man who entered the room. 'His wife, Halia, works for me as cook and housekeeper. Please sit down.' He indicated that she should take a seat at the table. 'Would you like wine or a soft drink?'

'Water is fine, thank you.' The need for a clear head was imperative, but perhaps it would be better if she got blind drunk, Louise thought wildly. At least then she would have no recollection of the night with Dimitri that was to follow.

Joseph had disappeared, but returned almost immediately to serve dinner. The roast lamb cooked with herbs and served with potatoes and vegetables smelled tempting and she suddenly discovered that she was ravenous. Was it only the previous evening that she'd had dinner with Dimitri in Paris? She had been so intensely aware of him that she had only picked at her food. So much had happened in the space of twenty-four hours.

The memory of what had happened during some of those hours made her blush. Dimitri undressing her and laying her down on the huge four-poster bed, stripping off his own clothes and stretching out beside her on the satin sheets, bending his head to her breasts and teasing her nipples with his tongue…

She choked and quickly took a gulp of water.

'Are you all right?'

She could not bring herself to look at him. 'Fine, thank you. The food is wonderful.'

Against the odds she enjoyed the meal, but afterward her tension returned. Through the French windows she could see the moon gleaming silver against the black sky. It was late in the evening, and she assumed that soon Dimitri would want to take her to bed.

'Would you like dessert or coffee?'

Caffeine would not help the ache that was rapidly becoming a throbbing pain across her brow. She gave him a lightning glance, unaware of the faint desperation in her eyes. 'Actually, I wonder if you would show me to my room? I have some headache tablets in my case.'

'Of course.' Dimitri rose from the table and led her out of the room and up the sweeping staircase. He strode along the landing, halted to open a door and ushered her inside.

The suite of rooms comprised a sitting room which led through a big square arch into a bedroom. Like the rest of the house the rooms were luxuriously decorated, with champagne-coloured silk wallpaper, pale gold carpets and curtains, and sofas covered in a darker gold silk brocade that matched the bedspread.

Louise did not need to see the jacket slung over the arm of a chair, or the squash racket and sports bag on the floor, to tell her that this was the master suite. She stiffened when she noted her suitcase standing by the bed.

'This is *your* bedroom, isn't it? I know we have an…arrangement…' She flushed hotly as she thought of the terms of that arrangement. 'But I assumed I would at least have the privacy of my own room.'

'I didn't deem it necessary,' Dimitri said blandly. 'As you pointed out, we have an arrangement, the terms of which require you to share my bed every night. However, you do have your own bathroom.' He crossed the room and opened a door to reveal a shower room and walk-in wardrobe. 'This is for you, but there is a bath in my *en suite* bathroom which you are welcome to use.' He glanced at his watch. 'I have a couple of calls to make, so I'll leave you to settle in. But I won't be long.' His green eyes glinted with amusement at her rebellious expression. 'Make sure you wait up for me, *glikia.*'

Panic gripped her. Last night she had been swept away by passion, but tonight the idea of getting into bed with him, having sex with him, seemed so cold-blooded. 'Is it too much to ask that I be allowed to spend this one night alone? I have a headache,' she said tightly.

There was no hint of sympathy in his smile. 'Then you'd better hope that your painkillers work quickly. I'll be back in half an hour.'

How on earth had she fallen in love with him seven years ago? Right at this moment she could happily murder him. 'You bastard,' she said shakily.

For long moments after he had gone Louise continued to stare at the door he had closed behind him, desperately tempted to flee the room, the house, *him.* The feel of soft fur rubbing against her leg made her look down, and with a little cry she stooped and lifted Madeleine into her arms.

'I've made a pact with the devil,' she whispered, 'and I have no choice but to see it through.'

The cat purred softly and then sprang down and walked elegantly over to the windowsill where, Louise saw, a cushion had been placed for her.

She watched Madeleine leap onto it and sighed ruefully. 'I'm glad *you* feel at home, anyway.'

Fifteen minutes later she had scrubbed off her make-up, brushed her teeth and hair, and donned the tent-like nightshirt she had packed. Dimitri was in for a shock if he expected to find a glamorous sex-siren in his bed, she thought with grim satisfaction as she studied herself in the mirror. The nightshirt was old and comfortable and reached past her knees. She looked more like a maiden aunt than a temptress.

In fact she could not bring herself to get into the huge bed after she had drawn back the bedspread and discovered that he slept on silk sheets. Instead she stood by the window, staring out at the dark garden and listening to the seconds on the clock ticking past relentlessly.

'Your choice of nightwear is not quite what I had envisaged,' a voice drawled, making her start.

She swung round to discover that Dimitri had entered the suite and was strolling towards her, his footsteps muffled by the thick carpet. He moved with the silent grace of a panther and was far more threatening to her peace of mind. He had discarded his jacket and undone his shirt almost to the waist. The sight of his darkly tanned chest covered with a fine mat of dark hair set her pulse racing.

She despised herself for her weakness and said sharply, 'You might have forced me into your bed, but you can't dictate what I choose to sleep in.'

Dark brows winged upwards. '*Forced*, Louise? There is no lock on the door to keep you here, nor chains to bind you. You are free to leave whenever you like.' He studied her thoughtfully. 'To be honest, I'm growing tired of being made out to be some kind of villain. We are two consenting adults who made a deal.'

He pulled a sheet of paper from his trouser pocket and handed it to her. 'I spoke to my lawyer a short while ago, and he sent an e-mail to confirm that he has already begun proceedings to purchase Eirenne. The money should be in your bank account within a week.' He paused and speared her with a hard look. 'But I can easily stop the process if you have changed your mind?'

Tomorrow her mother would be on her way to the specialist cancer hospital in America. Changing her mind was not an option, Louise acknowledged. She drew a swift breath.

'I want the sale to go ahead.'

The moonlight slanted over Dimitri's face, highlighting his sharp cheekbones and resolute jaw. He was arrogant and uncompromising, but the predatory gleam in his eyes told her that his desire for her was something he could not control. She sensed that he resented it, just as she resented her fierce attraction to him. They were both trapped by sexual need, and she gave a little shiver as she remembered how Dimitri had stated his intention to slake his hunger by making love to her until his unwanted fascination with her had faded.

'In that case you won't need this.'

Before she could stop him he gripped the hem of her nightshirt and dragged it over her head. She knew she was blushing, but she refused to give in to the temptation to cover her breasts with her hands and instead lifted her head proudly.

'*Thee mou*, you are beautiful.'

As Dimitri studied her naked body his breath hissed between his teeth. Louise was startled to see streaks of colour flare on his cheekbones.

'You were lovely seven years ago, but now you are beyond compare,' he said thickly.

Don't, she wanted to cry out. She did not want to be reminded of the most incredible night of her life and have those memories sullied by the soulless coupling they were about to perform.

Dimitri captured her chin and stilled when he felt the betraying moisture on her skin. Irritation flared inside him. Did she really think he would hurt her or take her by force? Or was she playing mind-games? Trying to make him feel bad for wanting what she had given willingly enough last night?

'Why the tears, *pedhaki*? Am I really such an ogre?'

She could not have heard a faint note of hurt in his voice—not from a man who was as hard as nails and immune to emotions. And yet… Louise lifted her eyes to his face and for a second she glimpsed the younger Dimitri, who had made love to her with such tenderness seven years ago that she had wept with the beauty of it.

He traced his thumb over her lower lip. 'Are you afraid of me?'

'No,' she admitted honestly. At least she did not fear he would ever cause her physical harm. But she *was* scared of the way he made her feel—out of control and a slave to her fierce desire for him.

He did not seem convinced. 'I have never taken a woman by force—I find the very idea abhorrent. You chose to come to Athens with me,' he reminded her.

'I know.' Her tongue darted out to moisten her dry lips. 'I will abide by the terms of our arrangement.'

Louise tried to ignore a flicker of panic when he cupped her shoulders and drew her inexorably towards him. She had never noticed before that his olive-green eyes were flecked with gold. Like tiny flames, she thought, blazing with an intensity of need that lit the fire inside her. He lowered his head and brushed his mouth over hers, lightly at first, as if he was giving her the chance to pull back. But she sensed his hunger, felt it in his hands that shook slightly, and as he deepened the kiss and it became an erotic exploration of her mouth he demolished all her carefully erected barricades.

He moved a hand down to her breast and teased her nipple with his fingers until it felt tight and tingling. Sensation arrowed down to her pelvis, evoking molten heat between her legs, and with a low groan she parted her lips beneath his and kissed him back. Without taking his mouth from hers he lifted her and strode through to the bedroom, where he placed her on the bed.

She was exquisite, Dimitri thought as he knelt over her and ran his fingers through her hair so that her curls were spread across the pillow like a golden halo. The bedside lamps were turned low and bathed her nakedness in a soft glow that made her creamy skin gleam. Her limbs felt like satin beneath his fingertips as he explored every inch of her, like a blind man reliant on touch, determined to imprint the shape of her on his brain.

Her breasts were rounded, delightfully soft and voluptuous, and when he pressed his face into the valley between them he inhaled the delicate fragrance of lilies. He raised himself up so that he could kiss her mouth again. Desire was pounding a pagan drumbeat through his veins and he wanted her with an urgency he had never experienced with any other woman. But he glimpsed the faint wariness in her eyes, and the memory of what she had said a few moments ago taunted him.

'I will abide by our agreement,' she had told him dully, as if she had resigned herself to a terrible fate. *Gamoto!* His male pride was stung. He did not want a sacrificial lamb. He wanted the eager sex-kitten she had been at his hotel in Paris and he *would* have her, he vowed. He would tease and tantalise her with his hands and mouth until she begged for his possession.

With deft movements he shrugged out of his clothes and lowered himself onto her so that their naked bodies touched from head to toe. His rock-hard arousal jabbed against her belly and he heard her catch her breath when she realised the size of him. He slanted his mouth over hers and kissed her, slow and deep, drawing a response from her that fanned the flames of his desire.

His body was impatient for sexual release, but he forced

himself to slow the pace while he trailed his mouth down to her breast and captured the dusky pink nipple between his lips, caressing her until she cried his name. She arched her hips in instinctive invitation and he laughed triumphantly, transferring his mouth to the other breast, lapping her eager flesh with his tongue.

'Dimitri…please…' she whispered tremulously.

He liked the fact that she could not deny her need for him. He slid his hand between her thighs, and when he discovered the proof of her arousal his restraint cracked. Pausing only to don protection, he positioned himself over her.

'Ise panemorfi.' The words were torn from him as he stared into her sapphire-blue gaze. 'I have to have you now, *glikia mou.*' He discarded his pride and did not care that he had revealed the intensity of his need for her.

'I want you too,' she admitted, and the unguarded honesty in her eyes made Dimitri's gut clench. She was no longer playing games. Maybe she never had been, he thought. Maybe she had never stopped being the lovely girl Loulou, who had once given herself so sweetly to him.

And then his thought process was obliterated as he thrust into her and felt her muscles stretch to accommodate him, to draw him deeper into her velvet softness.

Something curled around his heart—a feeling of possessiveness that would have bothered him if he'd had time to dwell on it. But his blood was pounding in his ears as she matched his rhythm and moved with him, accepting every hard stroke that drove them both higher. She sobbed his name and lifted her hips, her body as taut as an overstrung bow, before he tipped her over the edge. She shook with the force of her orgasm, twisting her head on the pillows, and raked her nails over his shoulders.

Dimitri's control shattered spectacularly. 'Wildcat,' he groaned raggedly, and tumbled with her into ecstasy.

CHAPTER EIGHT

A LONG time later Dimitri eased himself from Louise, surprised by his reluctance to break the physical connection between them. Sex with her had been as amazing as it had the previous night, and he felt a surge of male satisfaction as he propped himself up on an elbow and idly wound a honey-gold curl around his finger.

'That was incredible, *glikia*. I'm beginning to wish I'd stipulated that you should stay with me for longer than a couple of weeks.'

He frowned when he realised he was actually serious. Not that he was contemplating anything long-term, of course, he reassured himself. He was happy with his life the way it was—uncluttered by the emotional dramas that women seemed so fond of. But he could not deny it would be easy to become addicted to Louise's potent sensuality.

He studied her face, still rose-flushed from the passion they had just shared, and once again he was struck by her beauty, and the curiously innocent air that evoked a primitive urge to claim his woman and protect her from harm.

'Perhaps we will have to renegotiate the terms of our deal,' he murmured.

Dimitri's words dragged Louise from the blissfully relaxed state that followed intense physical pleasure, and dumped her back into the harsh world of reality. A deal—

that was all sex with him had been. Yet foolishly she had
allowed herself to feel that it had been a complete union—
not only of their bodies, but of their souls. Clearly that had
not been the case for him. She swallowed the lump in her
throat and clung to her pride.

'We agreed on the length of time I would be your mistress,' she reminded him coolly. 'I trust you won't go back
on your word and try and force me to remain here for a
day longer?'

'So we're back to accusations of force, are we?'

His tone was soft, his anger controlled, but the warmth
in his eyes had died and Louise felt the sensation of an ice-
cube slithering down her spine.

'I didn't see any sign of your supposed reluctance to have
sex with me. In fact I gained the impression that you rather
enjoyed it—and I have the marks to prove it.'

He sat up so that she could see his back, and she gasped
at the sight of several red weals on his shoulders, where
she had raked her nails across his skin in the throes of feverish passion.

Her face burned with mortification. 'I'm sorry. I didn't
realise I had marked you.'

'I'm flattered you found me so exciting, *glikia*,' he
drawled as he lay back down and folded his arms behind
his head in a position of indolent relaxation.

He looked like a sultan who had just been pleasured by
his favourite whore, Louise thought bitterly. Her long and
traumatic day had caught up with her and she ached with
tiredness, but the prospect of sharing Dimitri's bed for the
rest of the night was too much to bear. In a strange way
sleeping with him seemed even more intimate that having
sex with him. If they were proper lovers she would snug-
gle up to him and rest her head on his chest, and he would
cuddle her as they drifted off to sleep.

Memories of the night they had spent together on Eirenne made her heart ache. They had fallen asleep in each other's arms that night, and had woken at dawn to make love again. But the situation between them now was very different from seven years ago. She was only with him because they had made a deal, and surely she had fulfilled her side of it adequately tonight.

She slid her legs over the side of the bed and remembered that her nightshirt was in the sitting room. During their wild lovemaking Dimitri had flung the silk top sheet to the floor, and she quickly snatched it up and wrapped it around her to cover her nakedness.

He frowned as she backed away from the bed. 'Where are you going?'

'If you have finished with me, I would like to sleep alone in my own room. I don't think it is an unreasonable request.'

Dimitri made no attempt to hide his impatience. He was tempted to pull her down onto the mattress and show her that he was far from finished with her. Her tangible tension and his sudden realisation that her composure was close to snapping prevented him.

'None of the guest bedrooms are prepared, and I'm sure you'd agree it would be unreasonable to expect Halia to make up a bed for you at midnight.'

'Well…then I'll sleep on the sofa.'

Louise flushed beneath his speculative look. She expected him to insist that she join him back in the bed, but after a few seconds of silence, he shrugged.

'Please yourself. I have an important business meeting in the morning and I need some sleep.'

And with that he settled back against the pillows and shut his eyes, as if he was supremely indifferent to where she decided to spend the rest of the night.

Half an hour later Louise shifted position yet again on

the sofa, trying to get comfortable. She had demonstrated to Dimitri that she was not his puppet, but for some reason her victory seemed hollow. The sofa's cushions were much firmer than a mattress, and her neck already ached from where she was using the armrest as a pillow. With a sigh she pulled the sheet tighter around her, wishing that the air-conditioning did not work so well. She was cold and tired and felt stupidly close to tears.

Something soft brushed against her hand as Madeleine sprang up onto the sofa and settled in the crook of her knees.

'In two weeks' time Tina will be responding to the treatment, Dimitri will own Eirenne and our agreement will be finished. I'll never have to see him again,' she told the cat, and wondered why that last statement did not fill her with satisfaction as it surely should.

Sunlight dancing across her eyelids roused Louise from the restless sleep that had finally claimed her just before dawn. She stretched, and winced as her aching neck and shoulders reminded her of the uncomfortable night she had spent.

'I trust you slept well?' Dimitri strolled out of his bathroom, dressed in a dark suit and white shirt accessorised with a navy silk tie. He looked impossibly gorgeous and energised to face the day ahead—in contrast to Louise, who felt as if she had been flattened by a truck.

'Fine, thank you,' she muttered, gritting her teeth as his amused smile told her he knew she was lying. She felt tired and irritable, and his arrogance riled her. 'I would like some measure of privacy while I am here. I'll ask Halia for some sheets so I can make up a bed in one of the guest rooms.'

'No, you won't,' he said implacably. 'Our deal was for you to spend every night in my bed. And I would appreciate it if you could start acting like an adult rather than a petulant child.'

Louise's temper simmered. The temptation to throw the marble paperweight on the coffee table at his head was so strong that she clenched her fists to stop herself from grabbing it. Instead she verbalised her frustration. 'You can go to hell.'

'And *you* can go back to Paris and find yourself another buyer for Eirenne. Because frankly, *glikia*, I'm getting tired of your martyr act.' Dimitri strode towards the door, anger evident in every taut line of his body. 'If you don't want to be here you are free to leave.'

He did not add that if she returned home he would not continue with the purchase of the island, but the unspoken threat hung in the air.

Louise bit her lip, panic surging through her as she realised she had pushed him too far. Why *had* she so deliberately antagonised him? she wondered. The truth, she acknowledged painfully, was that she wished he would take her in his arms and kiss her into submission. She wanted him to make love to her but her pride would not let her admit it.

'I *do* want to be here.' She pushed the sheet away and stood up from the sofa to face him, thankful that she had put her nightshirt back on after she had left his bed. 'It's just that I'm finding this hard,' she admitted. 'I've never stayed with a guy before. I live alone, with just Madeleine for company, and I'm not used to this level of intimacy or to sharing my personal space with someone else.'

'Are you saying you haven't had many other lovers?'

Dimitri was surprised by his curiosity. He never asked about his mistresses' past history—partly because he considered it bad manners, and partly because he wasn't interested. But he was intrigued by Louise. She responded to him so passionately during sex that he had assumed she was experienced—which was why her air of innocence at other times puzzled him so much. And then there was the question of her designer clothes and the diamond pendant that she had told him had been given to her as presents. He believed they had been gifts from a lover, but perhaps he was wrong.

'Not many, no.' Once again Louise's pride asserted itself and prevented her from admitting that he was her only lover.

'Why not? You're a very attractive woman, and I can't believe you haven't had offers of relationships.'

She shrugged. 'I'm not interested in having a relationship.' She sensed he was waiting for her to explain her comment, and after a moment she continued quietly, 'Throughout my childhood I watched my mother lurch from one affair to another. I was sent to boarding school at the age of eight, and I never knew at the end of term where I would be spending the holidays. Often I visited my grandmother, but after she died there was no alternative but for me to stay with Tina and her current lover. My mother usually lived in a luxurious apartment when she was some rich guy's mistress, but inevitably after a few weeks or months he would tire of her and end the affair. Then she would have nowhere to live, and we would have to stay in hotels or she would rent a cheap place—until she found another man to keep her.'

She gave Dimitri a fierce look. 'I vowed when I saw how my mother was treated by her lovers—like she was an object rather than a person—that I would never have casual affairs or be reliant on anyone.'

Tina Hobbs had no one to blame but herself, Dimitri thought grimly. He felt no sympathy for his father's mistress who, in his opinion, had been no better than a prostitute. But for the first time he appreciated how Louise's upbringing must have affected her.

Children were far more perceptive than most adults gave them credit for, he mused. From an early age Louise's views about men had been formed from witnessing Tina's experiences, and he could not blame her for being wary and mistrusting of all men—including him.

His anger lessened and he walked back across the room to her. 'And yet you were happy to have a relationship with me seven years ago,' he said softly.

Louise stiffened, not wanting to be reminded of how stupid she had been. 'I was young and gullible back then.'

He frowned. 'What do you mean by gullible? I have good memories of the time we spent together on the island.'

Presumably he meant that he had enjoyed making a fool of her and breaking her heart. Memories of how he had hurt her, and the river of tears she had shed over him, evoked a dull pain in Louise's heart. She wished she could leave and never set eyes on him again, but for her mother's sake she had to stay and somehow survive the next two weeks with her emotions intact.

'What happened between us was over long ago,' she said tersely. 'I'm not the naïve girl I was then. I agreed to be your mistress in return for you buying Eirenne, and I am prepared to do whatever you ask of me.'

Something about their past brief relationship clearly troubled her, Dimitri mused. It was true they had parted abruptly, and events immediately after Louise had left Eirenne had meant he'd been unable to contact her for months. When he had eventually tried she had not answered his calls and at last he had given up.

He wanted to get to the bottom of the mystery, but a glance at his watch told him he did not have time before his meeting with the CEO of a Russian export company, with whom he hoped to finalise a deal. Further discussion with Louise would have to wait until tonight. It seemed that she was still desperate for him to buy the island and had decided to stay and stick to the terms of their agreement.

'In that case, my first request is that you bin the granny gown,' he murmured.

Her nightshirt had a row of tiny, fiddly buttons down the front that would take far too long to undo. Instead he gripped the two edges of the shirt and yanked them apart, sending buttons pinging in all directions and evoking a startled cry from Louise.

'You...*Neanderthal*!' Her voice shook with fury. 'Now I have nothing to sleep in.'

He looked unconcerned. 'Request number two—no, let's make that a demand: you sleep naked. Your body is far too beautiful to keep covered up.'

Dimitri trailed his eyes slowly over her and lingered on her breasts. The heat in his gaze made Louise's skin prickle and to her shame her nipples jerked to attention and stood proudly taut, demanding his attention.

'I see that the air-conditioning is set a little too cool,' he drawled.

She flushed. 'I hate you.'

'Really?' He gave her a sardonic look. 'I don't think it's me you hate, *glikia*, but you resent the way I make you feel.' He cupped her breasts in his palms and smiled when he felt the tremor that ran through her. 'Sexual desire between two consenting adults is nothing to feel ashamed of.' He lowered his head until his breath whispered across her lips. 'You want me. And I sure as hell want you.'

She wanted to deny it, and hated herself for the heated desire that licked through her veins. Her heart thudded as she waited for him to close the tiny gap that separated his mouth from hers. She longed for him to kiss her, and he must have sensed her impatience because he gave a low, triumphant laugh before he claimed her lips with fierce possession.

The effect was electric. Passion instantly flared between them, white-hot and simmering with potent urgency. She might resent him, but Louise could not resist him, and she gave up the fight that she had never stood a chance of winning and sank against him as he deepened the kiss and it became intensely erotic.

He skimmed his hands over her body and caressed her breasts, then moved down to probe his fingers between her thighs and discover her slick wetness.

Everything faded from Louise's consciousness but her need for Dimitri to make love to her. She slid his jacket over his shoulders and ran her hands over his torso, tugged at his shirt buttons and pushed the material aside so that she could feel his satiny skin and wiry chest hairs beneath her fingertips. Her body trembled with a primitive need to take him inside her and she boldly traced the hard ridge of his erection straining beneath his trousers.

Dimitri muttered a harsh imprecation as he swept her into his arms and strode into the bedroom. He dropped her onto the bed and knelt over her, caught her wrists and held them above her head while he captured one dusky pink nipple in his mouth. He lashed the taut peak with his tongue and then transferred his lips to her other breast and sucked hard, until she gasped and arched her hips in mute invitation.

Louise was all he could think of—his hunger for her. She aroused a level of desire in him that he had never felt with any other woman and his body shook with the intensity of his need.

Yet something hovered on the periphery of Dimitri's mind. The Russian deal. The ten o'clock meeting that, if it went well, would mean job security for hundreds of his employees at Kalakos Shipping—that would enable him to offer employment to hundreds more people who were without work at this time of economic hardship that Greece was currently experiencing.

Duty. He could not ignore its demands, even though his body was craving sexual release.

Louise must have sensed his hesitation. She stared at him, her expression unguarded and increasingly wary, as if she thought he was rejecting her. The shimmer of tears in her eyes made Dimitri's gut clench.

'Dimitri, what's wrong?'

'Nothing, *pedhaki.*' He quickly sought to reassure her. He groaned. 'But my timing is atrocious. I'm due at a meeting this morning to finalise a deal which is worth millions of pounds to the company and, more importantly, which will secure jobs for thousands of my employees.'

Louise released a shaky breath. For a moment she'd been afraid that he was playing a cruel game intended to prove his dominance over her. She traced the deep groove of his frown with her fingertips. She had read the news reports about Greece's financial problems, and how successful companies like Kalakos Shipping were vital to the country's economic recovery. Dimitri carried a huge weight of responsibility on his shoulders. He had been groomed from a young age to take over Kalakos Shipping from his father. After they had rowed Kostas had threatened to disinherit his only son, but presumably he had later realised that Dimitri was the best person to head the company.

She gave him a rueful smile and tried to ignore the restless ache of unfulfilled desire that throbbed deep inside her. 'Then you should go,' she said softly. 'People are relying on you and you can't let them down.'

Dimitri drew a ragged breath and rested his brow on hers

while his body reluctantly accepted that it was not going
to be granted the release it craved. Another woman might
have sulked and accused him of putting business before
her. He'd had mistresses who had not understood that running the company his grandfather had begun sixty years
ago was more than just a job.

But never before had he resented the commitment
Kalakos Shipping demanded of him, and never before had
he been tempted to ignore his duty. It took all his will-
power to get up from the bed, and he felt a sharp pang of
regret when Louise sat up and tugged the sheet across her.

'I'm sorry,' he said roughly. 'I promise I'll make it up
to you tonight.'

Her eyes met his. 'I'll hold you to that.'

She was so lovely. Her shy smile tugged on his heart,
and he ignored the fact that he was running late and leaned
over her to give her one last, lingering kiss.

'Last night you were crying in your sleep.'

He ran a finger lightly over the smudges beneath her
eyes, remembering how he had been woken by a sound
some time around dawn and had gone to investigate why
Louise had made that harrowing cry. She had been curled
up on the sofa, fast asleep, but tears had slipped from beneath her lashes and he had been sorely tempted to wake
her and try to comfort her.

'You seemed to be having a dream that upset you. Do
you want to tell me about it?'

Louise shook her head. She hadn't been aware that she
had been crying, but now she recalled fragments of the
dream in which she had been searching for her baby. It
must be seeing Dimitri again and being reminded of their
past relationship that brought back memories of the
miscarriage, she thought unhappily.

She looked into Dimitri's eyes and felt a little pang inside when she glimpsed a gentle expression in his olive-green eyes that she had never seen before. For a moment she debated telling him about the miscarriage. But she had never spoken about it to anyone, and it hurt—even after all this time it still hurt so much to know that she had lost his baby. Her greatest fear was that he would not care, that he would shrug his shoulders and say it had been for the best because he hadn't wanted a child. She could not bear to hear him say that, when she had wanted their baby so very much.

'I...don't remember what I dreamed about,' she told him huskily. 'It was probably about a film I watched recently. Sad endings tend to make me embarrassingly emotional.'

Dimitri studied her speculatively, not wholly convinced by her explanation. 'If you have a problem that's bothering you I would be happy to try to help.'

'I don't—but you'll have a problem if you're late for your meeting.'

He still felt reluctant to leave her. As he walked into the sitting room to retrieve his jacket another thought suddenly struck him.

'*Theos!* It's the fifteenth today. I'm supposed to be holding a dinner party tonight, and my sister is bringing her new baby,' he explained to Louise, who had wrapped the bedspread around her and followed him. He raked a hand through his hair. 'I'll cancel.'

'No, you can't do that.' Louise bit her lip. 'I didn't know Ianthe had had a baby.'

She thought of Dimitri's younger sister, whom she had met a few times when Ianthe had visited her father on Eirenne. The visits had been awkward occasions, during which her mother had monopolised Kostas's attention and Ianthe had clearly been upset by the break-up of her parents' marriage. But despite that a tentative friendship had started between Louise and the Greek girl, who was a similar age to her.

'Her daughter is six weeks old,' Dimitri told her. 'Are you sure you don't mind about dinner? You might like to see the baby—Ana's a cute little thing.'

Louise felt a sensation as if a lead weight had dropped in her stomach. The subject of babies was always painful—especially so when her emotions were still raw after the dream. But she could not explain her fear that seeing Dimitri's sister's baby would open a deep wound in her heart and intensify her grief for the child she had lost.

She realised that Dimitri was waiting for her to reply. 'I'm sure the baby is lovely. And I'd like to meet Ianthe again.'

'Okay, that's settled.' He snatched up his briefcase, dropped a disappointingly brief kiss on her lips, and headed for the door.

'Will the dinner party be a formal affair?' Louise ran a mental check-list of the clothes she had brought with her to Athens and concluded that she had nothing suitable to wear. 'I didn't pack anything that could remotely be called evening wear. It's a pity, because I have several dresses at home that would have been ideal.'

Dimitri paused on his way out of the door. 'Like the dress you wore to dinner in Paris?'

His jaw hardened as he recalled the black Benoit Besson dress, and the elegant suit by the same designer that Louise had worn the previous day. He still hadn't discovered who had paid for her clothes. He told himself it did not matter. He did not want to believe that she was a gold-digger like her mother. But his curiosity about the mysterious benefactor who bought her haute couture continued to bug him.

Louise frowned, wondering if she had imagined the sudden curtness in his voice. He was probably thinking about his business meeting and did not want to be delayed by a discussion about clothes, she told herself.

'The suit I wore yesterday will be okay, won't it?' She'd suddenly remembered it was hanging in the wardrobe.

'It'll be fine.'

Dimitri strode out of the room without glancing at her again, leaving Louise to wonder what on earth she was going to do all day when she did not have her job to occupy her.

CHAPTER NINE

AFTER breakfast, which Joseph the butler served on the terrace, Louise spent some time exploring Dimitri's well-stocked library, and was pleased to find the latest thriller from an author she enjoyed. But although the plot was intriguing her day passed slowly. She was not used to having spare time. Her job at the Louvre was absorbing, and for the past few months she had gone straight from work to the hospital, to visit her mother.

Later that afternoon she phoned the hospital in Massachusetts and was reassured to hear that Tina had arrived and was comfortable. The specialist hoped to start the treatment the following day, and seemed optimistic about her mother's prognosis. Louise knew that Tina's chance of making a full recovery was not a certainty, but at least now she had a chance.

Even though she resented the condition Dimitri had imposed, she was grateful to him for agreeing to buy Eirenne. It was highly unlikely that she would have found another buyer who could have raised one million pounds so quickly. Being his mistress for two weeks was a price she was willing to pay for her mother's life, and as long as she remembered that he only wanted her body there was no danger that he would be a threat to her heart.

'Kyria Frobisher?' Joseph walked across the terrace to

where Louise was sitting in the shade of a parasol. 'Kyrie Kalakos has left a message to say that if you wish to swim in the pool there is a selection of swimwear in the summerhouse,' he said in Greek.

'*Efkharistó.*' She smiled at the elderly butler. The late afternoon sun was scorching and the idea of a swim to cool off was tempting.

Following the path that Joseph showed her, Louise discovered a huge pool surrounded by white marble tiles that gleamed in the bright sunlight. The air temperature felt even hotter here, and the tall pine trees that circled the pool area prevented the breeze from rippling the surface of the turquoise water.

The summerhouse was unlocked, and after a few minutes of searching she found a storage box containing several bikinis. Who had they belonged to? she wondered. She hated the idea that Dimitri had invited other women to his house. From the skimpy cut of some of the swimwear she guessed that his girlfriends were happy to show off much more of their bodies than she was.

She chose a plain black bikini which was more substantial than a couple of triangles held together with string, and once she had changed went back outside to dive into the pool. The feel of the cool water on her heated skin was bliss, and she swam for a while and then climbed out and lay on a sunbed, telling herself that she would only close her eyes for a minute...

'I hope you used sunscreen.'

Dimitri's voice dragged her from sleep and she lifted her eyelids to see him striding towards her. Her heart gave a familiar lurch when he sat down on the edge of the sunbed. He had changed out of his business suit into black shorts and a sleeveless tee shirt and looked unbelievably gorgeous. Louise knew there was a gym and squash court in the basement of the house, and guessed from his toned physique that he worked out regularly.

'You didn't, did you? You idiot—don't you realise how quickly your fair skin will burn in this heat?'

Gorgeous, but as bossy as hell, she thought ruefully.

'I'm not a child,' she reminded him. 'I've only been lying here for a minute.'

'Sometimes you act like one.' Dimitri skimmed his eyes over her slim body and thought how unbelievably sexy she looked in the halterneck bikini.

His frown faded and was replaced by a wicked glint that set Louise's pulse racing.

'But you certainly don't look like a child, *glikia*. You are a beautiful, sensual woman,' he murmured against her lips, before he slid his tongue between them and explored the moist interior of her mouth.

She responded to him with an eagerness that made him instantly harden. *His* woman—Dimitri frowned again as he felt a surge of possessiveness that was unexpected and unwanted. She *had* been on his mind all day, he admitted. Even during the meeting with the Russians he'd had to force himself to concentrate, and when he had taken his team of executives for a celebratory lunch he'd been impatient to race home and take Louise to bed.

He trailed his lips over her shoulder. 'You've caught the sun. I love your freckles.'

'No, really? Do I have freckles?'

Her horrified expression made him smile.

'Uh-huh. There's one here.' He kissed her cheek. 'And here.' He kissed the tip of her nose. 'And here...' He trailed his mouth lower.

'I don't believe you,' Louise said breathlessly, when Dimitri finally lifted his lips from hers after a sensual kiss that left her aching for more. 'I haven't got freckles on my mouth.'

He laughed. Their eyes met—and time seemed to stand still. She remembered how they had been on Eirenne, the way he had teased her and made her laugh, the way he had kissed her until they were both shaking with need and he had carried her into the house in the pine forest and made love to her.

Desire unfurled inside her—a molten heat low in her pelvis. Memories of how they had almost had sex that morning flooded her mind and she leaned back on the lounger.

'You're back earlier than I expected,' she murmured. 'How was your meeting?'

'Successful—we finalised the deal.' Dimitri stroked his hand over her thigh and halted at the edge of her bikini pants. The tightening sensation in his groin was almost painful. Sexual awareness fizzed in the air. It was hot out here in the garden, and the temperature between them was rapidly rising to combustion point. The way she was looking at him made his heart slam against his ribs. There was plenty of time to make love to her before tonight's dinner party, he convinced himself.

He suddenly remembered that he had interrupted his journey home from the office to visit an exclusive boutique.

'I bought you this,' he said, handing her the box he had carried down to the pool. 'It's for you to wear tonight,' he explained as she sat upright and stared warily at the box, as if she feared it might contain a bomb.

Louise read the name of a famous Italian fashion house emblazoned in gold lettering on the lid. A sense of foreboding gripped her and despite the heat of the sun she shivered. 'I don't think…' she began.

'You won't know if you like what's inside unless you open it.'

Without another word she lifted off the lid, parted the tissue paper and took out a sapphire-blue silk cocktail dress.

The silence quivered with tension. If he was honest, Dimitri was disappointed by her unenthusiastic response. 'Do you like it?'

'It's exquisite.' Louise recognised that the dress was a masterpiece of brilliant design, and she had a fair idea of its price. 'It must have cost a fortune.' She carefully folded the dress and placed it back among the tissue paper, replaced the lid and held out the box to him. 'I can't afford a dress like this.'

'I don't expect you to pay for it.' His eyes narrowed when he realised she was serious about returning it to him. 'The dress is a present.'

'No, thank you.' Her refusal was instant and instinctive.

Memories from her childhood surfaced in Louise's mind. She pictured her mother, gleefully opening a box that had been delivered to a penthouse apartment in Rome owned by an Italian count. Alfredo Moretti had been short and balding, but he had also been immensely rich and Tina had become his mistress.

'Oh, my gosh! Black mink,' Tina had murmured reverently as she had lifted the fur coat from the box. 'Do you have any idea how much this must have cost?'

'It's not your birthday, so why did Alfredo buy it for you?' the ten-year-old Louise had asked.

Her mother had shrugged and continued to admire the coat in the mirror. 'I keep Fredo happy,' she'd said airily, 'and in return he gives me presents.'

Feeling slightly sick, Louise pushed the memory away. Dimitri looked surprised and annoyed by her violent rejection of his gift, but she could not help it.

'You don't have to buy me presents—and certainly not

expensive designer clothes. I'm sorry, but I can't accept the dress.'

He glanced at the box she was holding out to him but did not take it.

'But you accept expensive clothes from someone else,' he said, in a soft voice that for some reason made her shiver. 'You told me the Benoit Besson outfits I've seen you wearing were given to you as presents—I assume by a rich lover. Why won't you accept a gift from me?'

'That was different. Benoit gave me the dresses.'

'You mean you are *Besson's* mistress?'

Louise could not define the expression in Dimitri's eyes; it was somewhere between speculative and contemptuous. Her temper flared.

'Benoit is a friend,' she said tersely. 'I've known him for most of my life. When he was a fashion student I was his muse, and he designed all sorts of weird and wonderful creations. Then he became a successful designer, and sometimes he still likes to try out his ideas on me rather than at his studio. The clothes he gives me are those that he's made specifically for me—prototypes, if you like, for designs that are later modelled on the catwalk.'

'I see.' Dimitri relaxed a little, finally able to dismiss the ugly suspicions about her that had persisted in the back of his mind. But his satisfaction did not last long.

'*What* do you see?' Louise said sharply. She could see all too clearly what he had been thinking, and anger and hurt surged up inside her as the horrible truth dawned. 'You thought I had been given those dresses by wealthy men, didn't you? You thought—' She broke off, so furious that she could barely speak. 'You thought I was like my mother—that I was prepared to be some rich guy's mistress in return for material possessions. Is that why you thought I slept with you in Paris?' Her voice rose and she jumped up from the sunbed. 'Did you think that because you had paid for an expensive dinner you had *bought* me?'

Dimitri shrugged. 'You slept with me because you hoped to persuade me to buy Eirenne.'

Louise paled. His words hung in the air between them and she could not look at him.

'You wanted a million pounds as quickly as you could lay your hands on it. Isn't that right?' he continued remorselessly. 'But you've never explained why you need the money.'

'I don't owe you an explanation.' She stared at his hard face. The warmth she had seen in his eyes when he had teased her about her freckles had disappeared and she sensed that a chasm had opened up between them. 'I am *not* like Tina,' she said fiercely. 'She is my mother, and I love her, but I hate how she lived her life.'

She did not understand why she cared so much about Dimitri's opinion of her, but she desperately wanted to convince him that she was not like his father's mistress, whom he had so despised.

'The money is not for me. It's to help…someone I care about.' When he made no response she continued huskily, 'It was not the reason I slept with you in Paris. I did that because…because I—' She broke off and stared at him miserably, knowing she would be a fool to reveal the truth—that she had yearned to recreate the special night they had shared on Eirenne seven years before.

'Because what?' Dimitri demanded. He got up from the sunbed and walked towards her, his jaw hardening when she backed away from him.

'If it wasn't to persuade me to buy the island, why *did* you make love with me? Was it because you couldn't help yourself? Because you wanted me so badly that you couldn't resist me or deny your desire for me?'

Louise wished she could sink through the floor. She was utterly mortified that he had been aware of his effect on her. 'You arrogant bastard,' she choked. 'What do you want from me—blood or just my total humiliation?'

'I don't want either.' He gripped her shoulders to prevent her from fleeing from him. 'I'm telling you how it was for *me*. I was listing the reasons why I made love to you, *glikia mou*.'

She was too hurt to believe him. 'Don't call me that. You thought I was like my mother—and you once referred to her as a whore.'

Dimitri felt as if his heart was being squeezed in a vice when he glimpsed tears in her eyes.

'I was jealous,' he said harshly. 'When you told me your clothes had been gifts it seemed reasonable to assume they were from a man—and I was jealous. I *hate* the thought of you having other lovers—even though I know you must have done so in the seven years since you were mine.'

'You were *jealous*?' Louise gave a bitter laugh. 'What gives you the right, when you have a reputation as a playboy and your numerous affairs are plastered over the tabloids?' Her temper fizzed. 'Your attitude is *so* chauvinistic.'

'I'm not proud of the way I feel,' he admitted grimly. 'It has never happened to me before—this feeling that I'd like to kill any guy who comes near you.'

He was serious, Louise realised with a jolt. Dimitri looked as stunned as she felt by his admission. Her anger drained away and she shrugged wearily.

'I was never yours seven years ago. We spent a couple of nice days on Eirenne and slept together one night. We both know you only made love to me to get at my mother.'

Dimitri looked genuinely taken aback. 'Where did you get that crazy idea from?'

She ignored him as seven years of pent-up hurt burst from her like a torrent from a dam.

'I didn't stand a chance, did I?' she said bitterly. 'I admit I was painfully naïve for a nineteen-year-old—but, Goddammit, you took advantage of my innocence. You took my virginity without a second thought.'

Dimitri tensed at her accusation. Shock and another emotion he did not want to define but which felt disturbingly like possessiveness surged through him. He speared her with an intent look.

'You're saying I was your first lover? You told me at the time that you'd had other boyfriends.'

Louise flushed guiltily, knowing that she had not been entirely truthful with him. 'I'd been on a couple of dates with guys I met at university. But I'd never had a…a sexual relationship. I spent most of my teenage years at an all-girls boarding school and I hardly had an opportunity.' She sighed. 'Tina might not have been the most maternal mother, but she was very protective of me—especially with regard to boyfriends. I must have made it so easy for you.'

She cringed when she remembered how years ago she had fallen into Dimitri's hands like a ripe fruit ready for picking. In Paris, and again last night, she had fallen into his bed with embarrassing eagerness. Had she learned nothing? Where was her self-respect? she asked herself furiously.

Dimitri shook his head. 'The relationship we had on Eirenne had nothing to do with your mother. I don't know why Tina came out with all that rubbish about my motives, but I suspect it was because she disliked me as much as I disliked her and she was determined to turn you against me.'

'You can't deny you blamed her for your mother's death,' Louise said fiercely. 'Or that you held her responsible for your estrangement from your father. When Tina accused you of coming on to me because you wanted to get at her you admitted it. You said it was true. And then you…' Her voice fractured. The agony she had felt seven years ago was as acute now as it had been then. 'You walked away without speaking to me. You didn't even look at me. But why would you? I had served my purpose. You had riled my mother, and that was all you cared about—you certainly never cared about me.'

'I walked out because if I hadn't there was a strong possibility that I would have done something I would later regret,' Dimitri told her explosively. He took a deep breath. 'Look at me,' he commanded in a calmer tone.

When Louise refused, he slid one hand beneath her chin and forced her head up to meet his gaze.

'I swear the only reason I made love to you on Eirenne was because I couldn't help myself. I didn't go there with the intention of seducing you. *Theos*—' he made a harsh sound '—I went to the island to collect some of my mother's things that were still at the old house. She died two months before, but whether she meant to take an overdose of her sleeping pills or it was an accident we will never know. Certainly she was devastated when my father divorced her, but she did not write a note, and I can't believe she would have chosen to leave me and my sister.'

He lifted his other hand and brushed a stray curl back from Louise's face. 'When I saw you on the island my only thought was that you had transformed from a skinny kid into a gorgeous woman, and to be brutally honest I quickly became obsessed by my desire to take you to bed. The fact that you were the daughter of my father's mistress was irrelevant, and when we spent time together and I got to know you better I realised that you were nothing like Tina.'

Louise stared at him in shocked silence.

'After I stormed out of the Villa Aphrodite and my temper had cooled it occurred to me that you might have mis-understood what I had said,' he continued. 'I went back to talk to you—only to find that you had gone. I tore down to the jetty to catch you, but you were already on the boat and you refused to wait and listen to me.'

Dimitri's explanation of the events all those years ago sounded so reasonable, so believable, Louise thought shak-ily. Could she have been wrong and misjudged him? It was almost impossible to accept when she had spent so long thinking that he had cruelly used her. But he was staring at her now with a burning intensity in his eyes, as if he was determined to make her believe him—as if it mattered to him that she did.

She had been so young and unsure of herself, she re-membered. At nineteen she'd had no experience of men, and until she'd started university she had led a sheltered life at a convent school buried deep in the English countryside.

She had been overawed by Dimitri's stunning looks and easy charm, and amazed when he had shown an interest in her. Her lack of self-confidence had meant that it had been easy for her to believe her mother, and she had felt stupid for imagining that a gorgeous, sexy playboy could have desired *her*.

She was finding it hard to think straight when he was standing so close to her that she could feel the warmth of his body. The spicy scent of his aftershave teased her senses, and when she looked into his eyes and saw his gentle ex-pression her heart ached. She longed to sink against him and have him wrap his strong arms around her.

'How can I believe that what you've told me is the truth? That you didn't con me into sleeping with you? I saw you on the jetty as I was leaving the island, but I was hurt and confused and I couldn't bear to talk to you then. If I had mattered to you at all you could have contacted me. I'd told you I was studying at Sheffield University, and you had my phone number. But when I phoned you a few weeks later you refused to take my call. Your secretary said you were unavailable. You must have instructed her to tell me that,' she said accusingly.

Dimitri ran a hand through his dark hair. 'My PA told you the truth. I *was* unavailable. I was in South America with my sister—who was fighting for her life in an intensive care unit.'

Louise caught her breath. 'What happened?'

'Ianthe had gone on an adventure holiday in Peru and had been thrown from her horse on a mountain path, miles from civilisation. It took three days to transport her to the nearest city, and by then she had slipped into a coma. She had multiple injuries, including a broken neck.'

'Oh, Dimitri! Is she okay now?'

'Thankfully she made a full recovery, but it took a long time, and for a while the doctors feared she would not walk again. I lived at the hospital for weeks, sitting by her bed and talking to her. They said the sound of my voice might rouse her.'

Dimitri's expression became shuttered as he recalled the agonising wait and his desperate prayers that Ianthe would wake up and be well again. It had seemed unbearable that his beautiful, sport-mad sister might be confined to a wheelchair, and he was not ashamed to admit he had wept when she had eventually emerged from the coma and the doctors had confirmed that her spinal cord had not been damaged.

'I put my life on hold during that time. Your name was on the list of people my PA said had called me, and I did try to phone you from Peru, but to be honest all I could think about was my sister. My relationship with my father was still strained, but I spoke to him to update him on Ianthe.

He mentioned that you were doing well at university and I thought…' He shrugged. 'You were obviously getting on with your life. It seemed fairer to leave you alone—especially when I didn't know how long I would have to stay in South America.'

Louise cast her mind back to those dark days after she had lost the baby. Dimitri *had* called her and left a brief message with the number of his cell phone, but she had not tried to contact him again. In retrospect it was probably for the best that she hadn't, she thought heavily. He'd had enough to worry about with his sister. The news that she had miscarried his child would have been a shock when he had not even known that she was pregnant.

She ran her mind over everything he had told her. According to him he hadn't had an ulterior motive seven years ago but had genuinely been attracted to her. The tight knot of tension inside her loosened a little. If he hadn't played her for a fool, as she had thought all this time, was it possible that their brief affair had meant something to him after all?

'Louise, it was never my intention to hurt you. I can't pretend that I will ever feel anything but contempt for Tina,' Dimitri said harshly. 'I saw from the start of her affair with my father what kind of woman she is. But you are not responsible for her actions. I blamed her for breaking my mother's heart, but I blamed my father equally.' He sighed. 'We were both caught up in our parents' relationship and the fall-out from it, but it had no bearing on how I felt about you seven years ago.'

Louise's heart missed a beat. 'How *did* you feel about me?'

He gave her a rueful smile. 'That you were very lovely, and probably too young for me. After you left the island I couldn't get you out of my mind. But then Ianthe was injured and my place was with her. She needed me, and I was prepared to take care of her for the rest of her life if necessary. Seven years ago the time wasn't right for us to have a relationship. But now fate has conspired to make us meet again,' he murmured.

He was curious about the identity of this person Louise had told him she cared about. Evidently he or she meant a lot to her if she was prepared to go to the lengths she had to raise money for them. But was this person her lover? He couldn't believe it, Dimitri brooded. The way she responded to him made him certain that he was the only male in her life.

He wished she trusted him—but it was hardly surprising that she didn't after the lies her damned mother had told about him years ago. Trust was something that grew slowly as a relationship developed. But did he want a relationship with Louise that was based on any more than simply great sex?

'When you walked into my office a week ago I felt like I'd been poleaxed,' he told her roughly. 'You looked stunning, and if I'd followed my first instinct I'd have made love to you there and then on my desk. I couldn't forget you, and I used my interest in buying the island as an excuse to find you in Paris.'

Louise could not drag her eyes from Dimitri's face. His voice was so soft that it seemed to whisper across her skin like a velvet cloak, enfolding her and drawing her to him. Her heart thudded as his head slowly lowered.

'I'm glad you're here with me,' he said, and kissed her.

It was a slow, drugging kiss that stirred her soul. She could not resist him and parted her lips so that he could slide his tongue between them and explore the interior of her mouth until she trembled with need for him.

'I'm glad too.' The words slipped out before she could

stop them. But it was the truth, Louise acknowledged as Dimitri scooped her into his arms and laid her on the sun-lounger.

He knelt over her and she wound her arms around his neck to pull his mouth down to hers. This was the only place she wanted to be, and he was the only man she had ever wanted to be with.

The kiss became fierce and hungry as passion quickly took control. His hands shook as he untied the straps of her bikini top and pulled it down to bare her breasts.

'I want you, *glikia mou*,' he said thickly. 'I don't think I'll ever have enough of you.'

She watched him pull off his shirt and shorts and her mouth went dry as she stared at his naked bronzed body. He was a work of art—as perfect as a Michelangelo sculpture. Her eyes traced the dark hair that arrowed down over his powerful abdominal muscles and grew thickly at the base of his manhood. The size of his arousal made her catch her breath, and molten heat flooded between her legs when she saw the fierce intent in his eyes as he straddled her.

Soon he would be inside her. She arched her hips, impatient for his possession, but he smiled and shook his head.

'Not yet. Not until you are ready.'

He could arouse her simply with a look, with one of his sexy smiles, but the feel of his lips closing around one nipple and then its twin was so exquisite that she gave herself up to the mindless pleasure he was eliciting with his hands and mouth. Her heart thundered when he trailed kisses down her body. What he was doing seemed shockingly decadent when they were out in the open, with the hot sun beating down on them. But he slipped his hand between her thighs and gently parted her to explore her with his fingers and then his tongue, and the world disappeared as she became a slave to sensation.

'Louise…' Dimitri groaned when she reached for him and stroked the swollen length of his erection. 'It has to be now.'

Sweat glistened on the bunched muscles of his shoulders as he positioned himself over her. He had never felt like this before—so out of control. He wasn't sure he liked the feeling. He was used to being in command of himself and everyone around him. But when Louise smiled at him as she was doing now, with her eyes as well as her mouth, he felt—he felt that nothing in the world was more important than making her happy.

'Dimitri…' His name left her lips on a soft sigh and she looked into his eyes and saw the tiny gold specks dancing like flames. And then he thrust into her so powerfully that she gasped. But it was pleasure not pain that made her cry out, and as he withdrew almost fully and then thrust again she arched her back and welcomed each forceful stroke that took her higher and higher.

His woman… *His* woman. The drumbeat thundered in Dimitri's head and matched the rhythm of his movements as he quickened his pace. He was out of control, driven by a primitive need for this woman and only her.

Faster, harder…with each thrust Dimitri filled her—and Louise loved the way he moved inside her, making their two bodies one. She belonged to him—heart and soul. The thought floated into her mind as unobtrusive yet as tangible as a feather carried on a breeze.

And then he thrust the deepest yet and she stopped thinking, her entire being focused on the explosion of pleasure that detonated within her and sent shockwaves of sensation hurtling to every nerve-ending in a mind-blowing orgasm.

He came almost simultaneously. For a few seconds he fought it, but the intensity of pleasure caused by her internal muscles convulsing around him could not be borne for long, and he gave a savage groan as the tidal wave crashed over him and he felt the sweet flood of release pump from his body.

For a long time afterwards Dimitri could not move. He felt utterly relaxed, with his head pillowed on Louise's breasts, and he was reluctant to withdraw from her and break the bond between them. He hadn't had sex that good since—well, he couldn't remember when. *Maybe never,* whispered the little voice inside him. But it was still just good sex. There was no reason to think that the wildfire passion he had just experienced with Louise was anything more profound.

No reason at all, he reminded himself as he lifted his head from her neck and saw the sparkle of tears on her lashes.

'*Pedhaki*, are you all right? Why are you crying?'

Louise swallowed the tears that clogged her throat. She felt stupidly emotional and utterly overwhelmed. 'It's just… it was beautiful.'

Dimitri nodded. Beautiful was a perfect description. He couldn't have put it better.

CHAPTER TEN

'You look incredible,' Dimitri murmured later that evening, when he strolled out of his bathroom and caught sight of Louise wearing the blue silk cocktail dress.

'It's a beautiful dress.' Louise studied her reflection in the mirror and felt a little thrill of feminine pleasure as she acknowledged that she did look good. 'Thank you for buying it for me.'

She had agreed to wear the dress on the understanding that he would not give her any more presents. She believed him when he insisted he did not think she was like her mother, but the memory of Tina wearing expensive clothes and jewellery that had been gifts from her lovers strengthened Louise's determination not to accept anything from Dimitri. That way there could be no misunderstandings.

'My grandmother's diamond *fleur-de-lis* would have been the perfect accessory.' She voiced her thoughts unthinkingly.

Dimitri frowned. 'The pendant belonged to your grandmother?'

'Yes. My grandfather gave it to her as a wedding present. When she died she left it to me. I loved it because it reminded me of her.'

He had misjudged Louise badly, Dimitri thought guiltily. He had been quick to label her a gold-digger, but the truth was that she was nothing like her mother.

'You speak as if you no longer have it.'

There was a brief, awkward silence before Louise said quickly, 'It's at the jeweller's. The clasp was loose. Actually, that's where I went after I left your hotel in Paris.'

It was not a lie. The jeweller *had* told her that the clasp which secured the pendant to the gold chain was faulty and that he would have to repair it before he could sell the necklace.

Dimitri studied her intently, as if he guessed she was keeping something from him. 'It doesn't matter,' he said finally. 'You don't need any adornment. The colour of the dress matches the blue of your eyes just as I thought it would. If you would allow me to I would love to fill your wardrobe with beautiful clothes.'

'You said you like me best wearing nothing at all,' she reminded him with a wicked smile that set his pulse racing.

'That is true, and I will demonstrate my appreciation for your naked body later, *glikia mou*.' He laughed softly when she blushed. 'Anyone would think you were an innocent virgin,' he murmured, running his finger lightly down her pink cheek. 'But we both know that's not true.'

His kiss held tenderness as well as desire, and Louise melted into it, parting her lips beneath his so that his tongue could probe the moist interior or her mouth.

'I knew I should have cancelled dinner,' Dimitri growled, wondering how the hell he was going to get through the evening with a rock-solid erection straining against his zip.

Dimitri's dinner guests were personal friends rather than business associates. Louise sensed their surprise when they learned that she was staying with him, and was puzzled because she'd assumed that he often invited his mistresses to his home.

She did not like to think of herself as his mistress. Having seen her mother flit from one affair to the next, she had vowed that she would never give up her career and her independence for any man. Tina had treated the men she'd had affairs with like gods—but when they had tired of her they had treated her like dirt.

When her affair with Dimitri was over she would go back to Paris and the job she loved, and she would do her best to forget about him, Louise told herself, trying to ignore the way her heart lurched when he strode across the room towards her.

'My sister has just phoned to say she's running a little late,' he explained. Dimitri introduced the man with him. 'Louise, this is a good friend of mine—Takis Varsos. Takis is a curator at the National Art Gallery in Athens.'

'It is a pleasure to meet you,' Takis murmured.

He was a few years old than Dimitri, Louise guessed, pleasant-faced, with greying hair and brilliant black eyes behind heavy spectacles.

'I understand you work at the Louvre? I have many questions I'd like to ask you—and perhaps I can tell you about Greece's national art collection?'

Dimitri laughed. 'I'll leave the two of you to talk while I go and check that Halia is okay to delay dinner until Ianthe arrives.'

Fifteen minutes later Louise had finished a fascinating conversation with Takis when Dimitri rejoined her, accompanied by a dark-haired woman whose facial features bore a striking resemblance to his. She felt suddenly nervous, wondering if his sister resented her because of her mother's affair with Kostas Kalakos, but Ianthe greeted her warmly.

'Louise, I'm so pleased to meet you again. It's many years since we met on Eirenne, and there wasn't time for us to get to know one another,' she said without a hint of bitterness. 'How amazing that you and Dimitri met by chance in Paris.'

Louise flushed as she caught Dimitri's eye. 'Yes, it's a small world,' she murmured dryly.

'I'll get you some champagne, *agapiti*,' he told his sister, and strolled away.

'He's wonderful, isn't he?' Ianthe glanced after him. 'I was badly injured a few years ago, and he looked after me for months after I left hospital.' She looked curiously at Louise. 'I understand you are selling Eirenne to Dimitri? It will be nice to go back to the island. We loved it when we were children, and I would like to take Ana there for holidays when she's older.'

She turned towards the man who had come to stand beside her. 'This is my husband, Lykaios.'

Louise returned Lykaios's greeting, but her eyes were drawn to the tiny bundle wrapped in a shawl that Ianthe now carefully lifted out of her husband's arms.

'And this is our daughter,' Ianthe announced with fierce maternal pride. 'Ana Maria—which was my mother's name. I fed her before we left, so hopefully she'll stay settled during dinner. Would you like to hold her?'

She could hardly refuse. Louise hoped that if anyone noticed her sudden tension they would think she was simply nervous about holding a newborn baby.

Ianthe placed the precious bundle in her arms and she stared in wonder at the little face peeping from the folds of the shawl. Ana was beautiful, with a mass of black hair and petal-soft pink cheeks, her long eyelashes fringing huge dark eyes.

The pain in Louise's chest was so intense that she drew a sharp breath. It shouldn't hurt so much after all this time, she thought bleakly, but the loss of her baby was something she would never forget. A lump formed in her throat. If things had been different years ago she would have held her own baby in her arms, breathed in the evocative scent of her own newborn son or daughter. Dimitri would have been a father. But he was not even aware that she had conceived his child.

She wished now that she had told him—wished they could have shared the pain of losing their child. But perhaps he would not have cared. Perhaps he would have been relieved that her unplanned pregnancy had ended in a miscarriage.

The other guests had crowded round to admire Ianthe's baby and there was some good-natured teasing going on among the men about who was next in line for fatherhood.

'Dimitri's way behind,' Lykaios commented. 'He's not even married yet. You'll have to get a move on,' he told his brother-in-law. 'It's up to you to produce an heir to take over running Kalakos Shipping.'

'I don't think a child should be brought into the world to fill a pre-determined role.' Dimitri's tone became serious as lifted his niece from Louise's arms. 'A baby should be conceived from love, and if I ever have children I would encourage them to follow their dreams and live their life how they choose.'

Louise shot him a startled look. It was a bittersweet irony that his views on parenthood were exactly the same as hers. She'd felt instinctively that he would be a good father, and the tender expression on his face as he cradled Ana against his chest intensified the ache inside her.

She would *love* to have his child.

The thought stole into her head and refused to leave. It was stupid to think things like that, she reminded herself. After her first pregnancy had failed she had been warned that she might have difficulty conceiving again. And more pertinently, she must not forget that Dimitri had brought her to Athens so that she could fulfil her side of the deal they had made. She was his temporary mistress, and two weeks from now she would return to Paris and never see him again.

The guests had departed and the staff had returned to their own homes for the night. As Dimitri walked through the ground-floor rooms switching off the lights his thoughts were focused on Louise. She had seemed to enjoy the dinner with his friends, but beneath her smile he had sensed an air of sadness about her. He had even leaned close to her at the dinner table and asked if anything was wrong, and although she had assured him she was fine he had glimpsed a haunted expression in her eyes that bothered him.

The patio doors in the sitting room were open, the voile curtains billowing in the soft breeze. Louise was standing on the terrace and appeared to be absorbed in her own thoughts. She glanced up as Dimitri reached her and dashed her hand across her face—but not before he caught the glimmer of tears on her cheeks.

'*Glikia*, what's wrong?'

Louise shook her head, unable to explain the ache in her heart. If only she could turn back time…if only she hadn't listened to her mother and believed the worst of Dimitri… if only she hadn't lost their baby…

Regrets were pointless, but knowing it did not stop her wishing that things had been different.

Dimitri caught a tear clinging to her lashes on his thumb-pad and felt a strange sensation, as if a hand was squeezing his heart. '*Pedhaki?*'

'I was just looking at the stars and thinking how small and insignificant we are.' She laughed self-consciously. 'I think I must have had too much champagne.'

He knew she had only had one glass, but he said nothing and stared up at the black sky, pinpricked with millions of tiny diamonds.

'You see that bright star up there?' He pointed. 'That's the North Star.'

Louise stared at the heavens. 'Have you studied astronomy?'

'Not in great detail, but I used to go sailing with my father when I was a boy and he taught me a little of how to navigate using the stars. Of course GPS systems mean there's no need to look at the night sky now, but it was fun.' He sighed. 'I often wish I could turn the clock back.'

It was uncanny that they had both been thinking the same thing—almost as if their minds were connected, Louise thought.

'Why do you wish that?' she whispered.

'I regret that I was never reconciled with my father. Both of us said things that would have been better left unsaid, and I never got the chance to tell him that I was sorry, that I loved him. No one could have predicted his heart attack,' Dimitri said heavily. 'I was on the other side of the world when it happened and by the time I arrived back in Athens I was too late. He died an hour before I reached the hospital.'

'I'm sorry.'

Louise heard the raw pain in his voice and her heart ached for him. Dimitri had been estranged from his father because of Kostas's relationship with her mother, and although he did not mention it the spectre of the affair that had ripped his family apart hovered between them.

'It's not your fault,' he said gently, as if he had read her mind. 'None of it was your fault. I blame myself and my pigheadedness. I was young and arrogant. I saw everything in terms of black and white and forgot that life doesn't last for ever.'

Louise stared up at the stars. Sometimes life was over before it had even begun, she thought painfully.

'Dimitri—if what we had on Eirenne meant something to you, why didn't you try to contact me again later?' She tilted her head and studied his handsome face, felt the familiar dip of her stomach. His eyes were shadowed and she had no idea what he was thinking, but she had to ask the question that had been eating away at her. 'I know you couldn't at first, while Ianthe was in hospital, but after she had recovered why didn't you call?'

'I didn't for several reasons,' he said after a long silence. 'My damnable pride was one of them.' Louise had rejected him and it had hurt—although he had refused to admit it. He raked a hand through his hair. 'I wasn't in a position to contemplate any sort of relationship with you. My father had disinherited me and I thought—what the hell? I was angry and determined to prove to him that I didn't need him. I established my company, Fine Living, and worked obsessively to make it a success. I guess I needed to prove to myself as well as my father that I could make it on my own. My social life took second place to my ambition, and the women I dated were...'

'Were what?' Louise queried when he hesitated.

He shrugged. 'Women who knew how to play the game—who understood that all I wanted was an affair without emotional attachment. When my father died and I discovered that he had named me as his successor to head Kalakos Shipping after all I felt I needed to prove that I was worthy of the role.'

The long hours he'd put in at the office had left him with little time for anything else, Dimitri brooded. He had focused on work as a way of dealing with his grief at the death of his father. He stared at Louise. The moonlight had turned her to silver, and she looked ethereal and so very lovely that his heart clenched.

'My life was organised and under control until you stormed back into it.' He sounded almost angry. 'I thought I knew what you were—a common gold-digger who would sell your body for hard cash. I couldn't even blame you. How could you know any different when your mother had behaved that way? I told myself.'

He lifted his hand and wound a honey-blond curl around his finger. 'But you have proved my opinion of you to be wrong. *Thee mou*, we practically had a fight when I tried to give you this dress,' he muttered as he slid one strap down her arm and brushed his lips over her bare shoulder.

Louise could not restrain the little tremor that ran through her when he trailed a line of kisses along her collarbone. 'I'm sorry I reacted badly about the dress,' she whispered. 'And I'm sorry if I've disrupted your life.'

'I'm not.' Dimitri's voice deepened as he pulled her into his arms. 'I want to make love to you, but—' He broke off, thinking about the deal he'd made with her. He'd thought he could control her, like he controlled everything, but his plan had backfired.

'But what?' she said in a puzzled voice.

'But it has to be what you want too, *glikia mou*, and if it's not then you can sleep in your own room. I won't bother you or make any demands on you.'

Louise stared at him uncertainly. 'We have an arrangement…'

'I had no right to impose that condition on you. I'm *glad* to have the opportunity to buy Eirenne, and I will go ahead with the purchase whatever you decide about our sleeping arrangements.'

Her heart was beating so fast that Louise found it hard to breathe. She was still struggling to comprehend that

Dimitri had changed his mind and no longer expected her to be his mistress. He had given her a choice—and she already knew her answer.

'I want to share your room, your bed.' *Your life for ever,* she thought. For ever wasn't on Dimitri's agenda, but she would have tonight with him, and all the nights for the next two weeks. It would have to be enough.

He cupped her face in his hands and kissed her—a long, sweet kiss that sought a response she gave willingly. When he lifted her she wound her arms around his neck and rested her head on his shoulder as he carried her through the dark house and up to his bedroom, where moonbeams slanted through the blinds.

The sapphire-blue dress fluttered to the floor, followed by the wisps of her lacy underwear. Dimitri kissed her mouth, her breasts, and then knelt and trailed his lips over her stomach and the cluster of dark gold curls between her legs. He bestowed the most intimate kiss of all and dipped his tongue into her moist feminine heart until she cried out his name. And then he drew her down onto the bed and made love to her with fierce passion and an unexpected tenderness that brought tears to Louise's eyes.

'We really should get up.' Louise glanced at the clock the following Sunday morning and discovered that it was nearly afternoon.

'Why?' Dimitri murmured lazily as he pulled her closer to him and hooked his thigh over her leg. 'I'm quite happy here.'

'You said you needed to do some work today,' she reminded him. 'I feel I've already disrupted your schedule more than enough. You only went to the office two days last week. I don't want you to think you have to entertain me.'

He lowered his head and kissed the dusky pink nipple jutting provocatively above the sheet. To keep things fair he did the same to its twin, laughing softly when she caught her breath.

'I haven't noticed you complaining, *glikia mou*.'

'You've been a very attentive host,' she assured him gravely, and then giggled when he tickled her. 'Seriously, though, aren't you bored of staying at home? Joseph told me he's never known you to spend so much time at the house.'

'I haven't before,' Dimitri admitted. He rolled onto his back and drew her down on top of him. 'But I like being here with you.' His eyes gleamed wickedly. 'And I especially enjoy entertaining you.'

Louise gave up. She certainly wasn't going to complain about the attention he'd lavished on her. They rose late each morning and ate a leisurely breakfast-cum-lunch on the terrace. Dimitri usually disappeared into his study for an hour to catch up on e-mails, and then they would spend the afternoon by the pool—swimming, reading, and inevitably making love in the hot sun.

She loved simply being with him—just as she had all those years ago on Eirenne. The friendship they had shared then had been rekindled, as well as their passion for each other. She felt as though they were in a bubble, distanced from the rest of the world. But everyone knew that bubbles eventually burst, and she was aware that reality would soon intrude on their dream existence.

'I've just remembered I was going to take you to lunch at a great little restaurant I know in Rafina. It overlooks the marina, and I thought that afterwards I would take you out on my boat.' Dimitri kissed her lingeringly and groaned when she parted her lips beneath his. He rolled her beneath him. 'On the other hand, we could always go there for dinner this evening…'

* * *

The days sped past. Dimitri took her to the Acropolis and the Parthenon, and wandered patiently around with her when they spent a whole day at the National Gallery. Louise fell in love with Athens—especially at night, when it was cooler, and they browsed the shops that stayed open until late and visited lively tavernas.

Dimitri had given Joseph and Halia paid leave and arranged for them to visit their son, who lived on one of the islands. The couple deserved a break, he reasoned, and he had to admit that he liked being alone in the house with Louise. They could make love when they liked, where they liked. It occurred to him after a particularly erotic sex session on the sitting room carpet that he was fast becoming addicted to her.

Towards the end of the first week his lawyer had phoned to say that the sale of Eirenne was nearing completion.

'Once we have both signed the contract the money will be paid into your bank account,' Dimitri explained to Louise as he drove them to his lawyer's office. He was puzzled by her lack of enthusiasm. 'I expected you to look more pleased,' he murmured as they stepped out of the car.

'I *am* pleased,' she mumbled, unable to meet his gaze.

She knew Dimitri was happy to own the island, but she was sure he would be a lot less happy if she revealed that the money would pay for her mother's cancer treatment. He had every reason to hate Tina, she acknowledged miserably. She felt torn, her loyalties divided between two people she loved.

The thought was so shocking that she barely registered walking into the lawyer's office. *Love?* Where had that sprung from? She wasn't in love with Dimitri.

Her heart did that strange little lurch it always did as she studied his sculpted profile. She loved the sharp angles of his cheekbones and the sensual curve of his mouth, loved his unusual olive-green eyes with their fiery golden flecks—loved *him*, whispered that voice inside her.

He was everything, she admitted, and the realisation was terrifying—because she had vowed that she would never make a man the centre of her universe as her mother had so often done. She had promised herself that she would never fall desperately, madly, deeply in love—and she had broken that promise. She felt a sharp pain in her chest, as if an arrow had pierced her heart. Soon she was going home and Dimitri had given no hint that he wanted to continue with their relationship.

He arranged to take her back to Paris on his private jet, and on her last evening in Athens they had dinner at a charming little taverna, where they lingered over wonderful food and drank retsina before strolling home hand in hand.

He made love to her with fierce passion and exquisite tenderness, and although Louise told herself she had imagined it she sensed a faint air of desperation in his love-making that made her wonder if he regretted that she was leaving as much as she did. She felt that they had become close in recent days. But right at the start he had warned her he did not have a long attention span where women were concerned. Perhaps he had grown tired of her but was too polite to say so…

Unusually for midsummer, it was raining in Paris. The grey sky echoed Louise's mood, but Madeleine seemed pleased to be home, and when she was freed from the carrier she leapt up onto her usual windowsill, gave an elegant stretch, and then curled up and fell asleep.

'Your apartment was not designed for a person of my height,' Dimitri muttered as he forgot to duck and hit his head on the doorframe. 'Leave unpacking for now. I've got something I want to show you.'

She gave him a puzzled look. 'What is it?'

'You'll see. It's a surprise—one that I think you'll like.'

Mystified, she followed him back down to the car. 'Do you want another tour of the Louvre?' she asked a few minutes later, when the chauffeur parked opposite the Jardin des Tuileries.

'Come with me,' was all Dimitri would say, and he ushered her through the front door of a graceful old building that overlooked the famous gardens.

'Will you tell me what's going on?' Louise demanded as the lift took them upwards.

He grinned. 'Patience, *pedhaki*.'

They stepped out of the lift on the top floor. There was only one door on the landing, and Dimitri took a key from his pocket and opened it before standing back to allow her to precede him inside.

'What do you think?'

She looked around a huge, high-ceilinged sitting room which was beautifully decorated and luxuriously furnished.

'It's a fantastic apartment—especially with the view over the Tuileries. But why have you brought me here? Who lives here?'

'You do.' He laughed softly at her stunned expression. 'The agent left the key with the porter so that I could show you the place. If you like it I'll sign the lease and you can move in immediately.'

Louise stared at him, her mind whirling. 'I like the apartment I'm living in,' she said at last. 'I can't afford to move here. The rent must be astronomical.'

'Don't worry about that. I'll pay for all your living costs.' He ignored her frown. 'You must agree that your current apartment is too small for both of us.'

She caught her breath. 'Do you mean you want us to live

here together?' Her heart was beating a wild tattoo in her chest. 'Are you going to move to Paris?'

She watched him stiffen, watched his dark brows draw together, and her excitement trickled away.

'No,' he said slowly. 'You know I have to be in Athens to run Kalakos Shipping. But I'll visit you as often as I can. Why are you looking at me like that, *glikia mou*?'

Dimitri stared at Louise's wintry expression and felt a flare of irritation. What had she expected? He couldn't disrupt his life for her any more that he had already. He could not simply up sticks and move to France, and he did not expect her to leave her job and move to Greece. This was the best compromise he could think of.

'If you don't like this apartment there are plenty of others on the agent's books.'

'It's not the apartment. I mean, it *is*—but not in the way you think.' Louise felt sick with disappointment.

If she had any sense she would say nothing more and retain her dignity. Instead she discarded her pride.

'I thought when you said the apartment was for us that you were making some sort of commitment to me,' she whispered. 'I thought you wanted us to be together.' For a few heart-shaking seconds she had believed he cared about her.

He walked towards her, his frown deepening when she backed away from him. Women—he would never understand them, Dimitri thought grimly. He had thought he understood Louise, but now she was being irrational.

'Leasing an apartment for you—for us so that we can spend time together—is a kind of commitment.'

'No, it's not.' Memories of visiting her mother at the Italian Count's penthouse in Rome, or an apartment in Monaco paid for by a television celebrity who wanted to keep his affair with Tina secret from his wife flooded

Louise's mind. She would never give up her independence and allow a man to keep her.

'I refuse to be your mistress.'

'*Gamoto!* What have you been these past two weeks if not my mistress?' Dimitri demanded furiously.

He was tempted to shake her, but felt an even stronger desire to pull her into his arms and kiss her until she melted against him and they could end this crazy argument.

'I thought that we'd had fun these last two weeks. I thought you had enjoyed being with me just as I enjoyed being with you. Not just the sex.' He ignored her when she opened her mouth to speak. 'Everything—the companionship, the friendship we shared. What more do you want from me?'

His eyes narrowed as he realised that this was a familiar argument. He'd had it with several of his ex-mistresses. And it had always been a prelude to the end of an affair. Once a woman started talking about commitment it was time to head out of the door. So why wasn't he walking? Why did the idea of ending his relationship with Louise turn his mood as dull and grey as the sky outside the window?

'What were you hoping for when you said you thought I was making a commitment?' He gave a harsh laugh. 'Did you think I was going to *propose* to you?'

'No, of course not,' Louise denied quickly, her face flaming.

She hadn't expected that, but she *had* wanted some sign that she was more important to him than her mother had been to all those men who had used her and then discarded her when they'd grown tired of her. Dimitri setting her up as his mistress in an expensive apartment fell far short of the relationship she longed for. Maybe he had mistresses dotted around various European cities, she thought bleakly. No way was she going to join their ranks.

The sound of her cell phone made her jump. She quickly searched through her handbag, intending to cut the call, but the name of the hospital in Massachusetts on the caller display sent a chill of foreboding through her. The phone stopped ringing before she could answer it.

She glanced at Dimitri and bit her lip at his grim expression. He looked angry—and perhaps with good reason, she acknowledged painfully. Perhaps she had misjudged him and his motives for wanting to lease the apartment. She was just so scared of ending up like Tina that she was afraid to trust him.

'I need to return that call,' she told him flatly.

'Sure,' Dimitri spun round from the window and strode across the room. 'The driver is waiting downstairs and will take you home. I'll take the key back to the agent and tell him I don't want the apartment.'

He stared at her and felt a surge of frustration when he saw the undisguised misery in her eyes. To say that events were not turning out as he'd planned was a laughable understatement, but at this moment he had never felt less like laughing.

'I have to fly straight to Norway for a meeting I postponed last week.' It wasn't absolutely true. He had planned to spend the night with her here at the new place before leaving for his business trip in the morning. But he could do with some space, he thought grimly. He was angry that she had thrown the apartment back in his face.

He had enjoyed a lot more than simply physical gratification with Louise during the past two weeks, he admitted. But he had still regarded her as a mistress. He didn't want anything else. What was the point in commitment anyway? His parents had been married for thirty years, but their relationship had been blown apart by his father's affair and his mother had died heartbroken. Life was a lot simpler without emotions to screw it up, he thought sardonically.

Louise had followed him down the hallway to the front door. As he wrenched it open he glanced at her, and felt his heart clench when he saw the shimmer of tears in her eyes. So this was the end. He was shocked by how strongly he did not want it to be.

'Dimitri…' Her voice was choked, as if it hurt her throat to speak. 'I'm sorry.'

'So am I.' He wanted to kiss her, but knew that if he did he might make promises he did not know if he could keep. 'I'll call you.' It was what he always said when he ended an affair, but he knew damned well he wouldn't phone her. There was no point. They had reached a stalemate.

She moved past him. He watched her walk away from him down the hall. She did not look round as she entered the lift. The doors closed—and only then Dimitri realised that he was not ready to let her go.

CHAPTER ELEVEN

LOUISE's first priority when she arrived back in Paris from Massachusetts was to collect Madeleine from her neighbour.

'*Chérie,*' Benoit said gently as he studied her white face and hollow eyes. 'I'm so sorry about your mother. Is there anything I can do?'

She shook her head. 'Everything has been taken care of. I just need some time.'

She craved solitude. Her tiny apartment was a sanctuary and Madeleine a faithful companion who did not leave her side in the following days while she grieved.

At his office in Athens, Dimitri stared at the cheque for one million pounds that had arrived in the post and was now burning a hole on his desk.

During the past three weeks he had run through a whole host of emotions—ranging from anger when Louise had turned down the apartment he'd found for her in Paris to confusion, frustration and increasing fury when she had not answered any of his calls. In the last few days a feeling of dull despair had settled over him—a sense that all the joy had disappeared from the world.

That had changed when he had opened the letter addressed for his personal attention in Louise's handwriting and skimmed the brief note attached to the cheque. It explained that she was returning the full amount he had paid for Eirenne. There was nothing else—no explanation of her reasons, or indeed why she apparently wanted nothing more to do with him.

The lethargy that was so alien to him had been replaced once more by blazing anger. He deserved more than a pithy two-line note, he thought savagely. After three weeks of ignoring him, was that all Louise deigned to send him? No woman had ever ignored him before—and if they had he wouldn't have cared, he admitted. But Louise was different—or maybe it was he who was different? He had never felt like this before—as if his heart had been ripped out.

One thing was for sure: he was not going to allow her to ignore him any more.

He hit the intercom on his desk and growled like an angry bear at his PA. 'Arrange for the jet to fly me to Paris immediately. And cancel all my appointments—indefinitely. Please,' he added. Because in all fairness the mess he seemed to be making of his life wasn't Aletha's fault, and he felt guilty that she had been tiptoeing around him as if she feared his temper might explode.

Later that same day Dimitri stood in the hallway outside Louise's apartment and felt an uncomfortable cramping sensation in his gut. He couldn't wait to see her. Hell, he had missed her—he had refused to admit how much until now. But her note had given no indication that she missed him. There was every chance she would slam the door in his face when she saw him. He rang the bell and moved his foot forward, ready to jam it in the doorway.

He heard footsteps from the other side of the door and remembered her apartment had bare polished floorboards. The security chain was drawn back and then the door opened.

'Thee mou!' He could not restrain his shocked reaction. Her face was paper-white and there were purple shadows beneath her eyes. She looked at him dully, and her air of fragility tugged on his insides.

'Dimitri!'

She blinked, as if her brain had only just registered him.

'Glikia mou, what has happened?'

Louise drew a shuddering breath. 'My mother died.'

Dimitri felt a jolt of shock. It was hard to take in. Tina Hobbs—his father's mistress, the woman he had blamed for breaking his mother's heart—was dead. Seven years ago he had despised her, but now he felt nothing but pity for Tina. And for her daughter.

He stepped into the flat, remembering just in time to duck his head and avoid the low doorframe.

'Pedhaki,' he murmured gently, and drew her into his arms. She made no attempt to pull away, and as he stroked her honey-gold curls everything fell into place in his mind.

'When did it happen?'

'Two weeks ago.' Her voice was muffled against his chest.

He tightened his arm around her. 'Why didn't you call me? I would have come to you.'

The tenderness in Dimitri's voice brought tears to Louise's eyes. Her emotions were still raw, but she felt embarrassed that she had literally thrown herself at him. She eased out of his arms and led the way into the sitting room.

He looked gorgeous, she noted. Despite everything that had happened—especially her mother's death—she was blown away by the sight of him in beige jeans and a black silk shirt. The dark stubble on his jaw added to his dangerous sex appeal and her heart gave a familiar lurch.

'I tried to phone you many times but got no reply,' he said quietly.

'I was in America, and for some reason my phone didn't work there. I didn't contact you because…' Her voice faltered. She moved away from him and stood by the windowsill, absently stroking Madeleine. 'I couldn't after what happened the last time you were in Paris—those horrible things I said. You had found that lovely apartment for us, but I…I was too scared to accept what you were offering,' she said with painful honesty.

'It doesn't matter,' Dimitri assured her. 'I understand.' She'd needed to feel secure in their relationship, and at the time he hadn't appreciated how deeply her childhood experiences had affected her.

Louise bit her lip. 'There was another reason. I had done something awful.' Her voice shook. 'Dimitri, I sold you Eirenne so that I could use the money to pay for my mother's medical treatment. She had cancer, and her only chance was to have treatment in America. I didn't tell you because I knew you hated her and I was afraid you would pull out of the deal. You were my only hope—*her* only hope. Tina needed to start treatment immediately, and I knew you were keen to own the island and would push the sale through quickly.'

She paused, and then continued in a choked voice, 'In the end the money wasn't necessary. She wasn't strong enough for the doctors to try the treatment and she died in the hospital in Massachusetts. I was with her at…the end… and the funeral was held over there. I've always believed that your father should have left Eirenne to you, so when I came back to Paris I returned the money to you.'

'I received your cheque this morning.'

Louise's eyes flew to his face. His expression was unreadable, but she was certain he must be furious at her confession. Legally she had done nothing wrong, but morally—morally she had been torn between him and Tina, she thought bleakly.

She stared at the floor, tension spiralling inside her when she sensed him cross the small sitting room to stand in front of her.

'I knew while you were in Athens why you needed the money.'

He didn't look angry. He looked… She was afraid to try and define his expression. She shook her head, utterly confused. 'You can't have. How *could* you have known?'

He sighed. 'I was curious about why you were prepared to sell Eirenne for a lot less than it was worth. When you said you needed money quickly I wondered if you had debts, if maybe a loan-shark was hounding you for repayment. I didn't know what else to think,' he murmured when she gave a horrified gasp. 'I asked a private investigator to find out what he could. I wanted to protect you if necessary. But the investigator discovered that your mother was seriously ill and had been transferred to a specialist cancer clinic in the U.S. soon after I had agreed to buy the island. It wasn't hard to work out why you were so desperate for money.'

The room swam. 'Why did you go ahead with the deal once you knew the money was for my mother?' Louise said faintly. 'You hated her…'

'But *you* loved her.' He gave her a gentle smile. 'Faced with the same situation I would have done the same for someone I loved. I hoped you would trust me enough to tell me about Tina's illness, and when you didn't I felt that I couldn't mention it.'

He pulled her into his arms and Louise sagged against him, feeing too drained to understand anything any more except that Dimitri was here, holding her.

'I find it hard to trust,' she admitted thickly. 'I never

wanted to end up like Tina. She wanted to be loved, but when she was rejected by my father, and then by her lovers, she grew hard and used them like they used her.'

Louise's upbringing had left her with a ton of emotional baggage, and as a man who disliked emotions and kept his own under tight control Dimitri would ordinarily have run a hundred miles rather than get involved. But his life had been turned inside out from the moment she had walked into his office looking like a sex goddess in her short red skirt, he thought ruefully.

'Do you trust me, *glikia mou*?' He was conscious of the painful thud of his heart as he waited for her answer.

'Yes.' Simple, unequivocal. Louise knew she would trust him with her life.

'Then bring Madeleine and come with me.'

She did not even ask where he was taking her. It was enough to be with him.

Louise fell asleep on the plane. Dimitri carried her to the bedroom at the rear of the jet, laid her on the bed and tucked a blanket around her before he settled down with his laptop and fired off a few e-mails to his top executives. Kalakos Shipping was important, but Louise was more so, and he decided that it was about time he learned the art of delegation.

It was a short journey from Athens airport to the port of Rafina, where his boat was moored.

'Are we going to Eirenne?' she asked him as they sped out of the harbour and headed in a direction she remembered from years ago.

'Back to where it all began,' he said softly. There was a little more colour in her cheeks after her sleep, but the breeze blowing her clothes revealed she had lost weight, and she looked so fragile that his heart clenched.

The sun was low in the sky when they reached the island, a fiery orange ball that streaked the few wispy clouds to gold and bathed the path leading from the jetty in mellow light.

'Nothing has changed,' Louise murmured as they followed the path into the pine forest. She had mixed feelings about coming back to this place that held special memories but also regrets.

'I was surprised by how well Eirenne had been maintained,' Dimitri told her. 'It was only when I came here two weeks ago that I discovered your mother had employed staff to take care of the island and the two houses.'

The old house that had been built by Dimitri's grandfather was just as Louise remembered it. Half hidden among the pine trees, its many windows looked out over the sea that sparkled like a precious jewel in the evening sunshine.

Joseph and Halia greeted them at the front door. The couple were delighted with the staff cottage and happy to come to the island whenever they were needed, Dimitri explained as he led the way into the dining room. Louise couldn't remember the last time she had eaten a proper meal; her appetite had been non-existent lately. But the baked sea bass served with a colourful salad was delicious, and the crisp Chardonnay Dimitri served with the meal was a perfect accompaniment.

After dinner they sat on the terrace and finished the wine while the sun sank below the horizon and the air became filled with the song of the cicadas. For the first time in weeks Louise felt some of her tension leave her. She turned her head to study Dimitri's handsome profile and tried to ignore the ache in her heart. Nothing had been resolved regarding their relationship, but here on Eirenne she could pretend for a little while that everything was perfect.

'Thank you for bringing me here. I'd almost forgotten how beautiful the island is.'

'I haven't forgotten anything about this place.' He met her gaze, and in the shadows of dusk she saw the golden flecks in his eyes burning brightly. 'I remember bringing you to this house for the first time. I looked at you and thought you were more beautiful than any woman I'd ever seen.'

She gave a faint smile. 'That can't be true. You had been engaged to that stunning American model, Rochelle Fitzpatrick, but she had broken off the relationship. Perhaps you would have been attracted to *any* woman when you were on the rebound?' She voiced the doubt that still lingered.

Dimitri threw back his head and laughed. 'I wasn't on the rebound from Rochelle. If anything I was glad I'd had a lucky escape. Your mother was right about one thing— Rochelle did dump me when she learned that I'd fallen out with my father and I was no longer his heir. I realised that she was in love with the fortune she'd expected me to inherit rather than with me. I admit my ego was bruised, and I was disappointed with myself that I hadn't spotted her for a gold-digger, but I certainly wasn't heartbroken.'

'I see.' Another ghost had been laid to rest, and Louise's heart leapt when he stood up and stretched out his hand to her.

'Somehow I doubt that you do,' he said obliquely, but then he lowered his head and captured her mouth, and she was instantly lost in the beauty of his kiss.

The scent of the pine trees was evocative. Memories swirled in Louise's mind as Dimitri swept her up and carried her into the house. He set her down in the bedroom they had shared one night long ago, and undressed her and then himself. Pale fingers of moonlight gilded them, following the path of their hands as they explored each other's bodies. He kissed her breasts and her stomach, then knelt to bestow the most intimate caress of all, gently parting her thighs to dip his tongue into her honeyed sweetness.

When he laid her on the bed she reached for him and stroked his already hard arousal until he groaned and positioned himself over her. Their eyes met and held as he slid deep inside her, and when he began to move Louise thought that her heart would burst.

Four days later Dimitri woke at dawn and found that he was alone. Pausing only long enough to pull on a pair of denim cut-offs and slip something into his pocket, he walked quickly through the quiet house. The front door was open and he felt a flare of relief when he looked across the garden and spied Louise on the beach.

'That's the second time you've disappeared from my bed,' he murmured, remembering how she had left him sleeping at his hotel in Paris. He slid his arms around her waist. 'I don't like it, *glikia mou*. I've become addicted to waking and seeing your face on the pillow beside me.'

She gave him a faintly wistful smile. 'I was thinking that I need to go home. I've had almost a month of compassionate leave from work, but it's time to pick up the threads of my life again. My mother would want me to.' Her voice caught. 'She was proud of my career.'

Dimitri was conscious of a peculiar sensation in the pit of his stomach. Ever since they had arrived on the island he had been waiting for the right moment. And this moment, with the sun just rising above the pine trees and the sky streaked with pink and gold clouds that were reflected in the waves curling onto the shore, was the perfect moment.

'There is a job vacancy at the National Gallery in Athens

which Takis Varsos is very keen for you to accept,' he murmured.

Louise looked puzzled. 'At best it's a three-hour commute from Paris to Athens.'

'But if you lived in Athens…' He threaded his fingers through her hair and looked into eyes that were the colour of the sapphire hidden in his pocket.

If he asked her to be his mistress would she have the strength to refuse? Louise wondered. Should she throw away a chance of happiness because she was afraid of how she would feel when their relationship ended?

She was not her mother, she reminded herself. She was strong and independent and she was brave enough to live for the present rather than worry about the future.

'Commitment was something I had no interest in,' Dimitri admitted. 'I never understood how two people could know for certain that they wanted to spend their lives together. But then I met a golden girl who crept into my heart—and she stayed there, even though I didn't see her again for many years. Without realising it I compared every woman I met to her, but at last I understood and I knew that I wanted to be with her for ever.'

'Dimitri…?' Louise whispered. She had told him she trusted him. But she was afraid to trust the expression in his eyes, afraid to believe he could be saying what he seemed to be saying.

'I love you, Louise. You are my golden girl, the love of my life.'

Dimitri's hand was shaking as he felt in the pocket of his cut-offs and withdrew a ring—an oval sapphire surrounded by diamonds that sparkled in the brilliant light of the new day. He heard Louise catch her breath, and he captured her hand and lifted it to his lips.

'Will you marry me and spend the rest of your life

with me? Will you be the mother of my children? When I watched you holding my sister's baby something clicked inside me, and I imagined us having a child together—Sweetheart, what's wrong?'

Shock jolted through him as Louise snatched her hand out of his. She looked devastated. That was the only way he could describe her expression. And she was backing away from him, shaking her head.

'I can't,' she said in an anguished voice. 'I can't marry you. It wouldn't be fair.'

'*Theos!* I thought it was what you wanted—I thought, hoped…'

He must have been mistaken to think she cared about him. The realisation was gutting. For the first time in his life Dimitri was utterly floored. He couldn't think straight, and he felt a pain in his chest as though a knife had been plunged through his heart. *This* was why he had turned his back on emotions, he thought savagely. He had been perfectly content with his uneventful personal life that was never troubled by trauma and drama. But then Louise had gatecrashed his life and changed everything—changed him. She had made him love her and now he couldn't stop.

She had run down to the sea. For a moment he thought she was going to keep on running until the waves dragged her under, but she turned slowly to face him and he saw his pain reflected in her eyes.

'There's something I haven't told you. Something I should have told you.'

Fear made his voice harsh. 'Then for pity's sake tell me now.'

Louise drew a ragged breath. 'Seven years ago I fell pregnant with your baby. I was back at university when I found out, and I was shocked and scared, but…' She bit her lip, as if she could somehow hold back the emotions surging inside her. 'But I was excited too. I knew it would be difficult—I mean, it was totally the wrong time for me to have a child—but I wanted the baby...*our* baby. I loved it from the moment I knew it was growing inside me. I phoned you to tell you. I know now, of course, that you were in South America with Ianthe, but I assumed that you didn't want to have anything more to do with me.'

'*Thee mou,*' Dimitri said in a raw tone. 'I had no idea. I used protection—but nothing is one hundred percent effective. I should have checked you were okay after you went back to Sheffield, but I was angry that you had left me. And then Ianthe was injured and I was focused on her. But I did return your call eventually. Why didn't you tell me then? And the child...' The enormity of what she had revealed was only slowly sinking in. 'What happened about the baby?'

He watched her wipe her hand across her eyes.

'I miscarried in the seventh week of my pregnancy. Everything seemed fine, but then I woke up one day in agony. I was bleeding, and I guessed I was losing the baby.' Louise's voice shook as memories of that terrible day overwhelmed her. 'One of my housemates was a medical student. She suspected something was seriously wrong and insisted on driving me to A&E. I owe her my life. I was discovered to have an ectopic pregnancy, where the baby develops in the fallopian tube rather than the womb. The tube had ruptured, causing internal bleeding. Not only did I lose the baby, but the doctors had to remove my damaged tube.'

Intent on telling Dimitri everything, Louise hadn't noticed him move until she suddenly found him beside her. His expression was tortured and her heart turned over when she was that his eyes were wet.

'Louise, *pedhaki*—' His voice cracked. 'The thought of you going through all that alone, without my support, rips me apart. If I had known I would have come to you—even if it had meant leaving my sister. You needed me, and I will never forgive myself for not being there, not helping you through the grief of losing our child.'

'It happened so quickly. I was rushed into surgery and there wasn't time to contact you. Afterwards I didn't answer your call. I couldn't. I was so unhappy I couldn't bear to speak of what had happened, and it seemed pointless to tell you about a baby that I was no longer carrying.'

She touched his damp face and felt tears slip down her own cheeks.

'I love you,' she whispered. 'I always have. Through all the years that we were apart you lived in my heart and you always will.' She pressed a finger against his lips when he made to speak. 'I saw the tender look on your face when you held Ana. You would be a wonderful father, Dimitri. But I might never be able to give you a child. Even if I did fall pregnant there is a strong risk that I could have another ectopic.'

Dimitri brushed away her tears and cupped her face in his hands.

'I love you,' he told her fiercely. 'I will love you if we have children and I will love you if we don't. No one can predict what the future holds. Perhaps we will be blessed with a family, but if we're not we'll deal with it together. What matters is that you love me, my golden girl. And I adore you, *kardia mou.*'

He slanted his lips over hers and kissed her, and it was the sweetest, gentlest, most beautiful kiss because it was given with love.

'I want to fall asleep with you in my arms every night and see your face on the pillow next to mine every morning,' he said deeply. 'I want you to be my friend and my lover and my one true love. Will you be my wife, Louise, and stay with me for ever?'

'Yes,' she said simply—because no other words were necessary when her love for him blazed in her eyes. And her tears were tears of joy as he slid the sapphire engagement ring onto her finger.

EPILOGUE

A YEAR later, Louise sat with her sister-in-law on the terrace of the old house on Eirenne and watched Dimitri playing with his niece on the beach.

'I can't believe Ana is walking already. She's growing up so quickly.' Ianthe sighed.

'In a few months she'll have a little brother or sister and you'll be glad she's walking.' Louise studied Ianthe's bump with interest. 'I wonder if this baby is a boy or girl.'

'Lykaios and I don't mind. But it would be nice for Theo to have a boy cousin—they could play football together.'

Louise laughed and looked down at her son, who was sleeping peacefully in her arms. 'It's hard to imagine Theo running around—he's only eight weeks old.'

She stroked her baby's downy soft cheek and his shock of dark hair. 'I can't get over how perfect he is.'

'Or how tiny!' Dimitri had joined them, and crouched down beside his wife and baby boy. 'Look how small his fingers are. He's amazing,' he murmured, still awed by the fact that he was a father.

'He's our little miracle,' Louise said softly. 'Although he didn't seem that little when I gave birth to him. The midwife said he was a good weight for a first baby.'

She met her husband's gaze and her heart gave a familiar flip at his sexy smile. They had married a month after

Dimitri had taken her to Eirenne. The wedding in Athens had been the quiet event they had both wanted, attended only by close family and friends. Benoit Besson had made the bride's dress and had given her away in a simple but emotional church ceremony. Louise had carried a bouquet of fragrant lilies and had worn her grandmother's diamond *fleur-de-lis* pendant, which had been a wedding gift from Dimitri.

'When I realised you had sold it to raise money for your mother's treatment I scoured every jeweller's shop in Paris and eventually found it,' he had explained, when she'd stared tearfully at the necklace sparkling in a black velvet case.

Louise had been delighted to have the memento of her grandmother once more, but something that had made her even happier was Dimitri's decision to donate the one million pounds she had returned to him to the cancer research project at the Paris hospital where her mother had been a patient. She loved him more and more with each passing day, and knew that he loved her just as deeply.

She turned her head from him to watch Ianthe, who was lifting her daughter into the pushchair.

'I'll take Ana back to the villa for her nap. You two must come and see her nursery and the rest of the Villa Aphrodite now that the decorators have finished.'

'We'll be over later,' her brother promised.

When Ianthe had gone, Dimitri took Theo from Louise and settled him in his pram. 'He should sleep for a while yet, don't you think?'

'Probably—he had a good feed. Why? What do you want to do?' Louise's pulse-rate quickened when Dimitri swept her up in his arms and laid her on a sun-lounger.

'What I always want to do and will never tire of doing,'

he murmured as he unclipped her bikini top. 'I want to love you—with all my heart and soul.'

'And your body, I hope,' she whispered against his lips.

The golden flecks in his eyes blazed with love and passion and teasing amusement. 'If you insist, *glikia mou.*'

* * * * *

A sneaky peek at next month...

MODERN™

INTERNATIONAL AFFAIRS, SEDUCTION & PASSION GUARANTEED

My wish list for next month's titles...

In stores from 21st September 2012:

❏ Banished to the Harem – Carol Marinelli

❏ A Delicious Deception – Elizabeth Power

❏ A Game of Vows – Maisey Yates

❏ Revelations of the Night Before – Lynn Raye Harris

In stores from 5th October 2012:

❏ Not Just the Greek's Wife – Lucy Monroe

❏ Painted the Other Woman – Julia James

❏ A Devil in Disguise – Caitlin Crews

❏ Defying her Desert Duty – Annie West

❏ The Wedding Must Go On – Robyn Grady

Available at WHSmith, Tesco, Asda, Eason, Amazon and Apple

Just can't wait?

0912/0

& *Special Offers*

very month we put together collections and
onger reads written by your favourite authors.

lere are some of next month's highlights—
.nd don't miss our fabulous discount online!

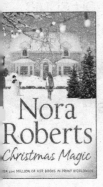

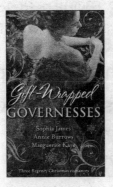

On sale 5th October   On sale 5th October   On sale 5th October

Find out more at
www.millsandboon.co.uk/specialreleases

Visit us Online

1012/ST/MB387